THE MARS TIME-PROJECT

ANTHONY N. FUCILLA

This book is dedicated to my daughter Kristina Elaine and my dear friend Gary Pope...

Published 2019 by arima publishing

www.arimapublishing.com

ISBN 978 1 84549 751 4

© Anthony Fucilla 2019

All rights reserved

This book is copyright. Subject to statutory exception and to provisions of relevant collective licensing agreements, no part of this publication may be reproduced, stored in a retrieval system, or transmitted in any form or by any means, without the prior written permission of the author.

This book is sold subject to the conditions that it shall not, by way of trade or otherwise, be lent, re-sold, hired out, or otherwise circulated without the publisher's prior consent in any form of binding or cover other than that which it is published and without a similar condition including this condition being imposed on the subsequent purchaser.

In this work of fiction, the characters, places and events are either the product of the author's imagination or they are used entirely fictitiously. Any resemblance to actual persons, living or dead, is purely coincidental.

Swirl is an imprint of arima publishing.

arima publishing
ASK House, Northgate Avenue
Bury St Edmunds, Suffolk IP32 6BB
t: (+44) 01284 700321

www.arimapublishing.com

THE MARS TIME-PROJECT

ANTHONY N. FUCILLA

Cover Design: Gary Pope, PJP Design
Editor: Vicky Cheyne Sheppard

Marcus Harlan has made Martian history... the first man to travel ahead in time. Upon his return he soon discovers that he has developed powers... powers to see into the future!

THE MARS TIME-PROJECT

The burning sun shone from beyond, casting its dim light across the colonised world that was Mars. Marcus Harlan stood outside his home on the arid desert ground, lapping up the thin, early morning air. He stretched his arms, sucked in oxygen and looked up into the blue terraformed sky, contemplating metaphysical notions of time travel...

"Marcus, breakfast is ready," cried his wife Charlotte from the open window as the warm summer wind swept across the landscape.

Out in the distance, Marcus caught sight of a big tractor bus trundling through the desert to town. Dismissing the scene, he briskly made his way into the large Martian hut and entered the kitchen. In the corner of the room was a circular tele-set. A live program was beamed to Mars from the night side of earth, blasted across space via an enormous number of megawatts... It was a documentary about Venus... The reception was good apart from some static... solar noise. The crackly roar of frequency...

"Time to get some breakfast down you," ordered Charlotte smiling, the hand on her hip brooking no nonsense.

Marcus sat at the breakfast table. Two boiled eggs and a lightly buttered piece of toast lay before him. He picked up his glass of mixed Martian fruit juice and swallowed. Licking his lips pensively, he said, "Charlotte, can I eat this later?"

A look of concern chased the smile from his wife's face.

"Marcus, what's wrong? Look, if you don't want to see this through..."

"Charlotte..." Marcus interjected softly, his brown eyes shining with muted clarity. "This will make history, Martian history. Besides, I'll be paid very handsomely..."

Charlotte shook her head, dismissive of the money...

"Just think," he pressed on, "the successful construction of the space elevator here on Mars made big news, but this...a journey into the future, the first man ever to journey in time. The news will spread all over Mars and beyond."

"So, it's the fame then?" She said, a little bitterly. "No don't answer that."

Her face softened with resignation as she sank graciously onto the seat beside him, her blue slavic eyes shining with emotion.

"I know it's not. It's something inside you. Something that you can't control, that makes you who you are."

"Marcus," she took his hand in hers. "If you feel compelled to see this through, then so be it... I..."

"Vegetables Mrs Harlan," cried a voice, husky with age from outside, shattering the moment.

"That's Mr Jones, the vegetable delivery man. He's here already..."

Charlotte rose to her slender feet and reluctantly went to open the door. After a moment, Marcus stood up and followed. As he walked out into the dim sunlight, he saw the familiar large grey surface-vehicle from which Charlotte was already selecting a vast array of Martian vegetables placing them into a basket. The vegetables themselves lay inside the back of the open vehicle in boxes. Martian flies circled, seeking moisture...

"Morning Mr Harlan."

"Morning Mr Jones," he replied with forced amiability. "Have you settled in yet?"

The short and chubby Mr Jones dusted down his trousers, fiddled with his cap and answered, "Still having trouble getting used to the weak gravity here to be honest. However, it certainly doesn't have any negative effects on the vegetables... I mean to say, they grow well here in the Martian soil, regardless. It's good stuff, everything you need for good leafy plants and healthy fat vegetables. Certainly keeps me out of mischief! Aside from that, I'm slowly adjusting to this new world." He grinned.

"It does take some getting used to. But you've made the right move Mr Jones. You certainly won't encounter any dangerous filoviruses here that's for sure. Besides your old home, Planet Earth has become way too over-populated and the one-world government controls its people like cattle. Out here you at least have a certain amount of freedom."

"You're right about that Mr Harlan. The laws on Earth have become so harsh, a man can't even breathe."

"Breathe being the operative word," snapped Marcus. "It's hard to believe you have to pay to just breathe back there. It's a sad state of affairs. You've heard that all Earthlings are totally mind controlled? The rulers even use music to control the masses."

"What do you mean...?"

"Well Mr Jones, there's an ancient dominant frequency which the human brain responds to. Remember everything breaks down into vibrations and that's frequency. If you incorporate that ancient dominant frequency into music, you can control both matter and thought. I've found it best to forget about the old world and its affairs..."

"You're right about that." Mr Jones paused, his eyes shifting from left to right. "Anyhow, one thing that I really do love about this planet is the 24-month calendar. One Martian year equates to two Earth years." His eyes now became distant and reflective as he counted on his fingers. "We are now in the month of July, the next month will be Zeno, followed by August, followed by Zeus. I think it's just great."

"That's right. You know the 24-month calendar has been well established for some time. Our forefathers were responsible for creating the Martian calendar which alternates between familiar Earth months and the newly created ones."

"Is that right? Tell me," asked Mr Jones curiously. "What was it like before the planet was terraformed, I mean before the oxygen project came into effect?"

"Well luckily I never had to experience it. By the time I was born, the planet had already been terraformed. However, bizarrely many of the early colonists who witnessed the change struggled to adapt."

"What do you mean?"

"Well, the early colonists got so used to wearing masks that suddenly, when they were no longer needed, many felt undressed going out without them..."

Mr Jones laughed. "Funny thing the mind hey..."

"Right," muttered Charlotte, breaking the flow of the conversation, the basket full... "I'm all done."

"That will be twenty, Mrs Harlan."

Charlotte generously placed twenty-five Mars dollars into his hand and graced the old man with a beaming smile, "Thank you Mr Jones."

"Thank you, Madam..." he tipped his cap in acknowledgement of her kindness. "All the best Mr

Harlan, until the next time...." He tipped his cap again, an earth habit of which he could not rid himself.

Marcus raised his hand, his thick gold ring shining in the Martian light. "All the best Mr Jones..." He turned pensively and made his way into the hut, Charlotte following behind...

It was night. The Martian gloom had fallen. Marcus sat comfortably in the dim light of a downtown bar sipping a small glass of Earth-imported red wine. The bar itself was an endless tide of sound and activity, filled with mutants chatting and drinking, some consuming the local brew which was, of course, synthetic. Many of the colonists had suffered the consequences of exposure to the deadly cosmic radiation that plagued the red planet. He started to reflect, thinking back to when his forefathers left Earth and journeyed to Mars, colonising and terraforming the alien sphere. They would first journey to Space Station X from which all interplanetary journeys started. Station X sat in orbit just over two thousand kilometres from Earth, circling the planet every two hours; a steppingstone to the stars. The impression of gravity was created by the centrifugal force produced as the station span slowly on its axis. In terms of daily life for the workers within the rotating space station, time didn't seem to exist. Night and day, months and seasons had no meaning. Once the ships had fuelled, they would wait for a precisely calculated moment. Then the motors would burst into life and the ships would pull away, out of the orbit in which they were circling, breaking free from Earth's pull and heading directly for Mars. The journey would take nine months. He began to recall what his grandfather had told him when he was a child, describing the experience of travelling to Earth, including the return journey home. The old man's voice came back to him now... *'Marcus, the experience of leaving Earth's atmosphere was exhilarating. From a thousand kilometres away, Earth was still very large, a jewel in space. At the centre of the disc the divisions between sea and land were clearly defined. In the cone of clear vision vertically beneath, the panorama was simply a spectacle. It was the ultimate spiritual experience...'* A waitress walked over, suddenly severing the flow of his thoughts.

She tried to surreptitiously slip a pill into her mouth. Her face was heavily emaciated. Marcus immediately understood why. She was taking amphetamines. This in turn caused hyperthyroidism, a condition where the thyroid gland produces too much of the hormone thyroxine. Her metabolism was working abnormally fast.

"Would you like some food Sir?" she said.

"I'm okay for now thank you," he replied smoothly.

The waitress turned and walked away, heading towards a group of mutants as they sat drinking, mumbling meaningless sounds.

"Marcus," said a voice from behind in casual greeting. "Mind if I join you?"

Marcus turned, and there standing before him was an old friend. He was a tall man, black hair, dressed in a one-piece green Martian suit and his piercing green eyes sparkled in the dim light.

"Hey Jeff... It's great to see you..."

Jeff made his way to the other side of small translucent table and sat, holding on to his cocktail.

"Great to see you too my friend... It's been in a while since we last met. Tell me, how's Charlotte?"

"She's fine," Marcus replied looking at him inquiringly. "How's Aurora...your lovely wife?"

Jeff wiped his mouth with a clenched fist and replied, "Aurora is up north at the moment. She went to see her mother in New Tokyo...She loves it up there. It's all those green parks. The local community has spent a lot of time tampering with and seeding the Martian soil. Anyway, Aurora is constantly trying to convince me to move there, but I like it here in the south. Once you pass the equatorial region of the planet heading north, I find the colonists to be quite rude, different to say the least. Anyway, as far as I'm concerned, our city Olympus is one of the best on the planet, period!"

"And what about your son...he must have completed his studies?"

"Yes! Would you believe Douglas is eighteen now? Even Martian years seem to fly by. He got top grades. Originally, he wanted to become a rocket-pilot but now wants to become a planetary economist. He's certainly got the brains. The only problem is he wants to complete his further education on Earth...reckons that their education system betters the one here by a gaping mile. He's got his eyes set on one of the top universities on Terra. Regardless, I'm trying to convince him to remain here on Mars and see out his education the Martian way. Besides his mother would be heartbroken if he made the move. Not to mention the tension that's grown between the two planets. Did you hear? All humans born on Mars are no longer classified as human by many down on Earth. We are considered as Martians, freaks, despite having the same biological and neurological essentials that make man. I've heard that immigration here on Mars is tightening up because of this. Earthlings that are considering a move to Mars might experience some problems!"

Marcus casually sipped at his red wine listening. "Yes Jeff, I'm aware of this. Earthlings...have closed

THE MARS TIME-PROJECT

minds and lack a universal understanding of what man truly is but, going back to education...Mars has a great education system now. Many of Earth's top scientists have moved here...nuclear-physicists, biophysicists, etc. Many of these great minds work within our academic system. There's certainly no need for your son to leave here, that's for sure... Not to mention that down on Earth, the government, the controlling power, brainwashes its people via the education system. They guide you through a scholastic tunnel: read this, listen to this, write this, I know, etc...At the end you come out with a piece of paper, semi-brainwashed, locked into their way of thinking. No real expansion of the mind. Here on Mars they teach you things in such a way that the mind is free to roam, to acquire without being brainwashed... But tell me my old friend, what about you? Are you still working with Cryogenics Inc...?"

"Indeed, I am," he said with some reverence. "I'm now head of the department. I manage a team of twenty... all ex-criminals that have been rehabilitated in the most nonconventional way."

"What do you mean?"

"The state has wiped out their personalities via neurological drug induced manipulation. These drugs alter the electrical patterns in the brain."

"I see," Marcus interjected. "It seems to me that even Mars has been somewhat infected by that mind control virus from Earth... Seems to linger throughout the cosmos... Regardless, I've not heard about this process, but as far as I'm concerned, personality is not all held in the brain."

Jeff smiled. "Let's leave that discussion for another time. Regardless, these people work well, very well in fact." He paused and rubbed his large, square, Teutonic jaw, then continued. "The other day we had a Mr Peter Howlett come out of his frozen state. He was basically a dead man who had waited for one-hundred years inside a coffin. Its outer shell held liquid nitrogen. There were clumps of cancer all through his frozen body. One-hundred years ago he was diagnosed with terminal cancer so he decided to be frozen hoping that one day in the future, medical science would find a cure. Well that's happened, we now have the cure. Frequency cures cancer. So, he's now come out of his frozen state and has reconnected with this existence. He's now legally alive."

"That's interesting...but what about the billions of cell walls ruptured by the expanding crystals of ice?"

"That issue has been dealt with. You'd be surprised at what medical technology can do today. So, tell me, what's happening with you?"

Marcus pushed back his blond hair and said softly, "I'm going to make history Jeff."

"History...? What are you leading to?"

"Have you heard of that agency, Quantum Effect?"

"Yes, I have. A group of scientists have made a revolutionary breakthrough in physics. They've built a Time-Machine, correct?"

"That's right Jeff..."

"Crazy if you think about it," Jeff replied. "But there's a fine line between genius and madness. They share the same genes after all... But what's this got to do with you? Tell me more Marcus..."

"Well, they have selected me to journey three hundred years into the future...the first man to ever journey in time...to travel in the fourth dimension."

"Are you serious?"

"Deadly serious...I was chosen because I'm considered to be one of the very best private detectives on Mars. They feel that I'm the right person to fulfil this mission...The government, which is led by several mutants, recommended me to the Quantum Effect agency. I was recommended by them because I had done some work for them... strictly confidential of course. Anyway, these scientists have chosen me, and it's now time for their invention to be put to the test and they believe that I'm the man to make it happen...Their motto is: the past, present and future is frozen in time and space. The implications are that we exist at different moments in this space-time continuum, and that the past, and the future, exist as much as the present."

"Now that's a little too metaphysical for me," laughed Jeff.

"Many scientists used to believe that the only way to journey into the future was to travel at the speed of light... an unimaginable velocity of 299,792,458 metres per second, but this invention has changed that..."

"Wow! This is ground-breaking Marcus, truly. But you must be somewhat fearful..."

"Fear is nothing other than a thalamic impulse Jeff...I'm a man of steel, it goes with my job as a detective."

Jeff looked a little sceptical. "But what about the risks involved?"

"In order to make history you need to take risks. Christopher Columbus and all the great Terra pioneers of the past would have agreed with me, including our forefathers who journeyed to Mars.

Man has always been frightened to venture into the unknown... besides I will be paid well..."

"How much...?"

"Let's just say an amount that will retire me..."

Jeff sat there sipping at his cocktail. He thought carefully before he spoke. "I see..." He paused. "Tell me Marcus, what tests have you had? I'm sure they would have examined you, testing your heart and general health, etc..."

"Oh yes," Marcus exclaimed. "I had a heart and lung test. I also had several blood tests taken. All was normal. They then exercised me close to exhaustion. After that, I was given a mini exam that entailed both arithmetic and psychology. During the exam I was placed in a tiny room too small for its purpose, just to add to the stress. Lastly, I was given certain puzzles to solve. It was timed accordingly. It all went well..."

"Well at least you weren't given an acute test in astrophysics...neutron stars, pulsars..."

Marcus regarded him with some amusement consuming his last drop of red wine.

"Tell me Marcus, if Quantum Effect can send you ahead in time, I assume that they can also send you back in time, correct?"

"No Jeff, that's not possible as paradoxical as it sounds..."

"What do you mean? That's inconsistent!"

"Jeff, it was all explained to me at Quantum Effect. You see, there are many major paradoxes related to backwards time travel...a contradiction in logic. Quantum Effect only deals with time-travelling into the future." Seconds of silence passed..."Picture this Jeff...If I was to journey back in time, my presence alone would alter history, the present, and in turn the future. I would start a never-ending time shift. A chain reaction...In other words, I would cause a fracture in time, creating another time-path. Thus, there would be inevitable changes throughout the course of time. This is known as chaos theory. In short, the notion of going back in time is peppered with many paradoxes..."

"I understand," Jeff muttered thoughtfully, absorbing the data given. "So, when is this journey of yours scheduled to happen...your historic journey ahead in time?"

Marcus glanced deeply into his eyes. His heart began beating faster as he contemplated his metaphysical journey. "Tomorrow..." He paused for a few seconds. "I have to be at Quantum Effect at 3pm. In fact," he glanced at his glowing triangular watch which lay fixed across his wrist and read the time: 10pm. "Jeff I need to make my way now. I'll catch a tractor-bus or M-cab. It's getting late..."

Jeff stood up smoothing down his suit with a slender hand and said, "Let me take you back Marcus. Jump in with me. I'll give you a ride..."

The small bulky surface-vehicle moved at pace whistling through the shifting red iron-oxide sands of the desert. Marcus sat inside gazing into the

Martian darkness. The stars were out, sharp majestic and dazzling. Soft curtains of aurora hung over the skyline. In the distance Marcus could see a canal, one of the many canals on Mars. Then suddenly, the beaming lights of the surface-vehicle captured a group of drunken mutants.

"These damn freaks," snapped Jeff, a vicious snap. "Most of them are unemployed. They spend their days drinking and seeking government support."

"Not all of them," replied Marcus. "It was a group of mutants within the government, operating at very high levels, that was responsible for putting my name forward to Quantum Effect."

"Yes, true. But the majority are a waste of space as far as I'm concerned. They should send them to Ganymede, especially now that the satellite planet is being terraformed. Apparently, there's liquid water under its surface...a saltwater ocean estimated at a drilling depth of 200km. They need all the help they can get out there."

Jeff suddenly accelerated then seconds later decreased their velocity as Marcus' hut came into view. He pulled up sharply with a low-gravity bump. Dust puffed up around the vehicle fading into the silent night.

"Thanks for the ride Jeff..."

"Pleasure my friend." Jeff eyes held deep reverence as he contemplated his friend's metaphysical journey. "I'm not sure what to say...only, please make sure you stay safe. I will look forward to your return...oh and please send my regards to the future Martian world." He smiled... a smile that brought a sense of jest to the seriousness of the challenge.

"Don't worry Jeff." Marcus' eyes widened with sudden importance. "I'll be in touch once I'm back in natural time."

They shook hands. Opening the door, Marcus stepped out and walked towards the hut. He placed his thumb across the reader and the door opened obediently. He entered briskly and made his way upstairs, heading to the bedroom where much needed rest awaited him.

The next day came too fast. To him, time passed in a flash. No sooner did he close his eyes than he had to open them, his dream-state seeming to last only seconds. Eventually, the clock struck one, signalling the end to a morning that passed without incident. It was almost time for him to depart and make his way into the city where he would reconnect with Quantum Effect. He sat in the kitchen, dressed in a one-piece white Martian suit, munching on a thick triple layered sandwich. Charlotte walked in halting by the sink.

"Are you all set darling?" Her eyes welled with sadness and concern. Even her brave smile wasn't enough to mask her burning fears.

"Yes," he replied his mouth half-full. He finished chewing and swallowed. Wiping his lips, he stood up and stepped towards her, his eyes blazing with importance. "It's time my love...time to make history. Your husband's name will be known throughout the solar-system and beyond..."

He kissed her on the forehead then hugged her tightly. She trembled against him, reluctant to let him go but reluctant to stand in the way of his ambition. Eventually she looked up into his eyes and seeing his resolution would not be swayed, she said, her eyes wet with tears, "You've always wanted the ultimate challenge. Well, it's waiting for you. I love you. Be careful."

Marcus made his way for the door. As he stepped out, he gazed towards the horizon thinking about the historic moment that was to come. In certain sections of the red iron-oxide desert, arid plants grew absorbing sunlight; Martian photosynthesis. He looked on, staring at the familiar sand dunes, dreamily recalling the days when he would climb them during the years of his youth. A soft wind tossed Martian sand dust into his left eye. Instinctively he raised his hand and rubbed, then briskly turned and walked towards the surface-vehicle shelter. The large shelter stood isolated and alone, several metres away from the hut itself. The hut was also isolated, their nearest neighbour being a gaping three miles away. As he pressed his thumb against the reader, the thick metallic door opened rapidly. He stepped in, opened his vehicle, and sat. After a few seconds of contemplation, he activated the surface-vehicle and drove out at pace...

Marcus Harlan stood outside the familiar dome, dwarfed by its immense size. He was suddenly overcome by a familiar inescapable excitement which was building up inside him. The dome glistened faintly in the afternoon light. It was located in the heart of the city of Olympus. It was only three weeks ago that he had met up with Quantum effect and been subjected to the various tests he had described to Jeff the night before. This was his second visit; the one that really mattered. Slowly he entered the dome and made his way over to the reception where the familiar young brunette stood slender and oozing elegance. It was eerily quiet.

"Greetings Mr Harlan, it's good to see you again," she said warmly, her green eyes filled with Martian dignity. "Professor Neal Clarkson will be down shortly. Please take a seat."

A shaft of sunlight came blasting through a window like a questing search light. It was momentarily eclipsed by a cloud, but the cloud soon passed, and sunlight shone again. As Marcus turned in search of a seat, Professor Clarkson came walking over. He was a middle-aged man, grey hair, withered face, dressed in a white lab-coat, and he moved with purpose.

"Mr Harlan, it's great to see you again." His voice was hard, professional and his eyes shone with brilliance. They shook hands. "Please come this way..."

They took an elevator and reached the second floor. Stepping out, they walked towards large metallic doors. Professor Clarkson pressed his finger on the reader, and the doors opened. Marcus saw yet again, the iron-coloured spherical-machine. It sat across a white floor shinning with brilliance. On his first visit he had spent some time gazing at it with cerebral ecstasy, touching it, overcome with a sense of historic significance. The mystique of time-travel he thought...

"Mr Harlan," said Clarkson briskly. "Before we prepare you for the journey, we feel it necessary to implant you with a very special device."

"What do you mean?"

"My colleague will explain more. Please follow me."

Marcus was led into a small office. A man that he had not met before sat at a large desk. He was partially bald, and his thick grey moustache stood out oddly against his pale skin and cold blue eyes.

"Mr Harlan, please take a seat... "I'm Professor Paul Molloy."

Marcus sat down, silently facing the man. Professor Clarkson remained standing, unconsciously rubbing his smooth jaw.

"Mr Harlan," said Molloy with a professional eye. "We have decided to surgically implant you with a time-recall-device, a backup system if you like. Of course, you will be paid extra if you comply...an amount of two-hundred thousand Martian dollars. Add that to the amount already due to you, the total becomes a handsome seven million Martian dollars...that will be enough to retire you, Sir, and some..."

A light film of perspiration covered Marcus's forehead. He was taken aback, concerned. This sounds like mind control at an extreme level, he thought. "Please explain," he muttered.

"This tiny time-recall device will be surgically implanted into your brain. It will be inserted into the region of the brain known as the hippocampus. The hippocampus is a complex brain structure. It's embedded deep in the temporal lobe. It forms an important part of the limbic system. In short, the hippocampus regulates memory, in particular, long-term memory."

Clarkson now stepped in and said, "Mr Harlan, the time-device operates like this..." He moved towards the desk so that he was facing Marcus. "The eye is a camera...it forms an image of the outer world on the retina, and then transmits it to the brain. This time-recall-device has the capacity to collect and store all data, i.e. visuals and sounds via the brain's memory bank..."

"Why is this necessary?" asked Marcus, his face darkened with curiosity.

Clarkson replied briskly, "Mr Harlan, as you know there are minor risks journeying through the fourth dimension. Very minor, but we do need to consider them."

"Yes, minor risks... death or potential lobotomy. I guess that's why I'm being paid so well."

"In short," said Molloy, now re-establishing his part in the conversation. "In the event something was to go wrong once you return to natural time...we would still be able to collect all the data from the time-recall device, all the images of the future, sounds, etc. It's the ultimate backup system..."

"I assume that the time-device will be removed upon my return, regardless?"

"Of course, Mr Harlan, that goes without saying..."

"Fine..." Marcus said running his smooth hand across his face in thought. "How long will it take you to implant this time-device in my head...?"

"Once sedated, an hour." Molloy's eyes grew wide. "Well, are you happy to proceed Mr Harlan?"

A cold silence fell... Marcus was silent, numb for a time. Although delighted to be the first man to travel ahead in time and make history, the idea of having this device implanted in his head concerned him. It reminded him of the mind control tactics that were practiced on planet Earth. However, given the circumstance, he clearly understood the reason and logic behind it. If I want to do this, I must accept, and proceed accordingly, he thought bitterly... Marcus gazed at the floor and then looked up and said, "I must confess, I'm somewhat perturbed by the idea. However, I accept... Whatever you feel necessary to ensure that history is made."

"Great... Now, with regard to your journey three hundred Martian years into the future, just to remind you again, we will be responsible for your return into natural time. An hour from the moment of your departure, you'll be brought back into natural time. It's a brief journey into the future but a significant one..."

Sometime later, Marcus awoke on a hygiene bed dressed in a white glossy robe. He was expecting to feel drained and dull, but it was quite the opposite. Suddenly he heard footsteps. Molloy and Clarkson came walking over with the head technician who had been responsible for the implantation.

"How are you feeling Mr Harlan?" Molloy muttered softly, his eyes fixed on him with distinct positivity. He tapped his right knee lightly.

"I'm feeling fine...energised."

"Good, that's what we expected to hear. The time-device was implanted with great success." Clarkson said slightly smugly, smiling with a beaming confidence, a confidence that transmitted courage but then an element of shrewdness crept into his smile. "Everything went according to plan. Well, once you are dressed, we will take you through."

"I hope everything else goes according to plan," replied Marcus. "I mean my journey, and my return."

"You are in good hands Mr Harlan... The overwhelming probability is that all will be well. Think positive. The odds are in your favour."

Marcus rose up and got to his feet with heightened colour in his cheeks. He stretched then rubbed the left side of his head where the incision had been made expecting to feel a bruise, scare or bump, but detected nothing. Calmly he made his way over to where his one-piece white Martian suit lay, thinking about his journey, a journey that would change the course of history...

THE MARS TIME-PROJECT

Marcus stepped into the time-chamber. Its sides were perfectly round. A hidden device took a beta-wave shot of his brain. An electric eye....As he sat down on the black seat, adrenalin flooded through him. Above his head and within reach, long tubes of bright light pulsed. For a flicker of a moment he felt dizzy. It was purely psychosomatic. He then started to think about his wife and the possibility of death. His hands clenched into fists of remembrance. Perspiration surfaced around his face. His heart was pounding. His mind began to work, piecing together memories into a collective semblance of chronological order. He pictured all the beautiful moments that they had shared from when they first met up until now... He shook his head and refocused on the task. He knew the risks involved, but his desire to make history nullified all such memories and potentially imposing fears. He moved the smoothly working lever forward and within a matter of seconds he was overwhelmed by a roar. He began to twitch and move spasmodically. Portions of his skin began to quiver, then darkness - the darkness of no-time. Shifting textures of destiny flashed before him and at once he entered the scattered flow of time. He was now moving within the depths of a dark seemingly endless tunnel at a velocity that could only be defined as supernatural... Then Marcus found himself standing in the Martian desert. The sun had dropped behind the horizon. The landscape was briefly illuminated by the Martian sunset. I'm three hundred years in the future, he thought in complete amazement. He briefly recalled his grandfather's words concerning the nature of time...' *The experience of time, Marcus, is the experience of observation. Time is your medium of perception and is the fabric on which your life's story is written. It is the experience of one moment that is constantly changing.*' Then, in the distance, he could see lights, a city, and the city was spectacular; a futuristic city that resembled something from another galaxy. Even from a distance, he could see that it was something extraordinary. With burning curiosity, he started to jog, then run, twisting and turning spasmodically...eyes filled with hunger and awe...then...

"Mr Harlan, can you hear me?" Clarkson said smoothly.

A merry dazzle of light awoke him, as Clarkson shone a pencil beam torch into his right eye.

"Yes, yes I can," he mumbled blearily.

"Congratulations Mr Harlan," snapped Molloy as he slowly approached the hygiene bed. "You've made history. You are the first man to have travelled into the future..."

Marcus opened his eyes. His vision was blurred as he battled to register with reality. He rubbed his eyes and slowly full clear vision was restored.

"What... what happened? I barely recall anything...The last thing I remember was sitting in the time-chamber moving the lever forward and then darkness. My last memory was that I was travelling through a dark tunnel at a tremendous velocity...that's it!"

"Don't worry Mr Harlan, we expected this," said Molloy sharply. "We are not surprised at all. The psychological effects of moving through time are vast, that's why the time-recall device was inserted into your brain. You have suffered memory loss as a result of the sudden transition from one reality, a future reality...back into your reality...the current world, natural time. Your mind has taken a serious pounding. However, we have removed the time-recall device and seen what was necessary. Again, congratulations Mr Harlan...You have proven that our invention here at Quantum Effect works. You have made history...and are now a rich man."

Seconds of silence passed...

"Please, tell me, what did I see?"

Without making a reply, Molloy activated a switch which was located against the wall beside the bed. From the foot of the bed itself, a large rectangular screen slowly rose and then halted. Within seconds images appeared... He could see himself standing in the Martian desert as the sun dropped behind the horizon. Suddenly, the images sped up into a blur of energy. Then natural flow was resumed. He could now see himself standing in a majestic futuristic city. A swirl of spectacular buildings lay ahead, immense, colourful and seemingly metallic. Martian citizens roamed back and forth chatting

THE MARS TIME-PROJECT

and gesticulating, dressed in elaborate, multi-coloured suits. Then he could see himself gazing up into the atmosphere looking at a slick black hover-car. The mechanics of life, he thought as he sat on the hygiene bed, his emotional equilibrium returning...Further on he could see a large dome. Molloy suddenly deactivated the switch and the images faded and the screen withdrew.

"That's pretty much it, Mr Harlan," said Molloy eying him narrowly.

Clarkson now interjected.... "You spent a full hour in the future Mr Harlan. You should be a proud man. Tell me, have the images jogged your memory in any way?"

"No nothing at all. As I mentioned, the last thing I recall was travelling through a dark tunnel at a tremendous velocity, that's it."

Marcus rose to his feet unsteadily, feeling heavy and sluggish; as if he had gone from zero gravity and had to adjust suddenly to the weak Martian gravitational pull. The images that he had just seen exploded in his mind, like the ultimate revelation...

"I'm one of the great pioneers..." he said with distinct pride, his eyes brightening.

"Yes Mr Harlan, indeed...you've etched your name into history, universal history," replied Clarkson. "With regard to your payment, the credit transfer has already been made. Seven million Martian dollars is now in your account."

Molloy swiftly interjected, "Mr Harlan we recommend that you remain here overnight and rest. You can leave in the morning..."

"I think it's wise to remain here," Clarkson said re-emphasizing the point.

"Yes, I agree," replied Marcus. "I feel quite drained."

"Indeed, you would. You've taken quite a battering both emotionally and psychologically," muttered Molloy... "Get some rest..."

THE MARS TIME-PROJECT

The next day came fast. Marcus had spent the night at Quantum Effect and had slept well. He was on his way home still feeling somewhat weak, jaded. He had just spoken to Charlotte via the surface vehicle's phone system, telling her of his success and his extraordinary experience. He had also informed her of the full amount of Martian dollars that had been paid to him...an amount of seven million. He had checked his account accordingly via the surface vehicle's computer system. He couldn't wait to see her. He now switched on the radio via the aid of a slender button, seeking relaxation. There was static but that promptly faded. He kept the volume low. He could hear a dim voice. It was the ubiquitous Professor Gregory Dawkins discussing Newton's third law of motion. It was the science channel which he was well accustomed to. He now increased velocity and within no time he was driving past the huge Mars spaceport. He could see rockets taking-off, heading into the vast desert of the inner solar-system. Hydrogen and oxygen were combusted for rocket propulsion. Most of the hydrogen was imported from Titan, one of Saturn's moons. As a result, Titan's economy was flourishing due to the mass sale of hydrogen mined from its atmosphere. Then a little further on he saw the Mars-based radars which were used to discover asteroids. Powerful computers would calculate their orbits: all data and information were then stored. From the strength of the radar-echo, asteroid diameters were attained. He dismissed the scene briskly and refocused on his journey, keeping his eyes wide and alert.... Within no time he was home. He placed his thumb across the reader and the door opened.

"Charlotte," he called out eagerly, walking into the kitchen. There was a jerkiness about his movements. He halted and the proud light in his eyes shone bright.

Without a word she turned away from the sink of dirty cups and dishes and skipped over. She stretched out her arms and held him tight as a beam of Martian sunlight shone through the open window illuminating the couple with exact precision.

"I'm so glad you are back and well my dear husband." She paused with emotion..."Your days working as a private detective are over." She pictured the seven million Martian dollars with great delight. "Tell me, have the dollars been transferred into our account yet?"

"Yes. The transfer was made yesterday. It's safely in our account. It's a new life for us now." He kissed her tender lips, pressing her close to his body, so much so that he could feel her heartbeat.

Charlotte smiled with contentment. "We can buy one of those huge Martian domes near the lakes and live there... You can buy yourself a new surface vehicle, and the rest." She paused as her imagination wandered around materialistic gain... "But tell me all about your trip in time. You must surely remember something?"

"Charlotte, I've already explained this to you...I recall nothing." He cut off sharply, trying to avoid getting into a technical argument.

"But surely..." She regarded him with some consternation.

"Charlotte, I really don't recall anything other than travelling through a dark tunnel at a tremendous velocity. Once in the time-chamber, I moved the lever forward then darkness...that's all I remember. However, as I said, I got to see the images second hand via that time-recall device. The time-recall device revealed it all with startling accuracy I might add. It was a strange feeling watching myself standing in a desert three hundred years in the future, next gazing at a futuristic city...I can't explain it..."

He stood there, and all at once a strange feeling came upon him, one he had not encountered before. He felt a wave of dizziness. Charlotte noted the sudden transition in his face.

"Sweetheart, are you ok?

"Yes, he mumbled... "I think I need to rest..."

With wide, concerned eyes she guided him to a chair and went back to the sink, occasionally throwing concerned glances his way but trying to give him some peace and quiet. Marcus sat at the breakfast table, rubbing his head, the sounds of ordinary everyday life helping him to regain his mental balance. On the table lay a newspaper. There was an article about the dangers of Plutonium. Marcus glanced at it and read: *Plutonium when inhaled can cause lung cancer.* He read on... '*Plutonium taken into the body moves quickly to the bone marrow...There is no way to stop it; the victim will die. Neutrons from the metal tear through the body, ionising tissue, transmuting atoms into radioactive isotopes, ultimately destroying and killing.*' He pushed the paper aside dismissively. Then there was a loud knock. Charlotte made her way to the front door and opened it. A tall well-dressed man stood there, holding a black folder. He was a middle-aged, his hair a mix of black and grey.

"Good afternoon Madam... my name's John Short, I'm from the Mars Daily..."

Charlotte interjected sharply... "You're a journalist."

"Yes, Madam...I am sorry for the inconvenience, but the fantastic story of your husband's historic journey in time has filtered through. Quantum Effect has released this great news to the media and public at large. I'd love to be the first to interview him, if I may." He smiled an ingratiating smile...

"How did you find our address?"

"You'll be surprised what journalists are capable of..."

"Hold on," she said, walking away.

As she entered the kitchen, Marcus looked up rubbing his head wearily.

"Who is it?"

"It's a journalist from the Mars daily. He wants to interview you?"

"Already...?" His voice cut through the thin Martian air with surprise and evident annoyance. "Tell him to leave a card. I'll contact him next week sometime..."

"Okay she replied," darting towards the door with purpose...

THE MARS TIME-PROJECT

Hours passed. It was now seven pm. Marcus was lying in his bed, eyes open, fully awake. That strange feeling still lingered. He battled to shake it off, but it wouldn't leave, irrespective of his lying down in a relaxed mode. Suddenly, as if space and time had opened up before him, and the world he knew had faded from his sight, he saw images of his friend Jeff and his son Douglas. The images shimmered in an oscillating haze, but were still clear, sharp and distinguishable. They continued to dance in the forefront of his mind as he lay frozen on the bed, his eyes wide, and arms flung aside as if dead. He could see his friend and his son at the spaceport. They were leaving Mars and heading to Titan, one of Saturn's moons. 'Destination Titan' pulsed in green across the departure board. Next he could see the ship leaving Mars with an acceleration so great that it was in outer space almost at once...Next he could see all the passengers relaxing in the pseudo-gravity of the ship including Jeff and his son Douglas, then the two pilots sitting in the control-room, making all the routine checks and corrections. Then he heard sound, a white noise; a roar that ranged through all frequencies. Destruction followed. The ship blew apart... For a moment, the area around the exploding ship was no longer a vacuum, given the outpouring of oxygen from the ship. The explosion in space looked like a brief spherical burst of light moving outwards. The little remaining bits of debris from the explosion were forced outward in every direction from the centre of the blast, and continued to move in a straight line without any atmospheric force to stop it. Suddenly the images dissipated like a fading cloud of smoke and the ceiling above, which had temporarily vanished, was restored to clear view. Marcus's face dripped with sweat. His body shook. His heart pounded as he battled to understand what had taken place. Then, he heard footsteps. Charlotte entered the bedroom with a light springy step...

"Marcus, surprise...! Jeff Mikkelsen is here. He wants to see you. He's going on holiday tomorrow with his son Douglas... destination Titan..."

Marcus went dead white... He sat up as adrenalin flooded through him...His heart pumped hard.

"What's wrong?" his wife said with concern, looking into his troubled face.

With a delayed response he mumbled, "Tell him to come up..."

Jeff entered the room holding a one-dollar Martian coin. He flipped the coin into the air gleefully. It glinted as it spun and came down in his outstretched palm, succumbing to weak Martian gravity. He said, "Marcus, you've made history my friend. Your name is echoing everywhere."

"Indeed, I have," Marcus replied, eyes restless.

"That Professor Paul Molloy and Professor Neal Clarkson from Quantum Effect were interviewed. I watched it on the news. I know exactly what occurred... the time-recall device, etc." He paused and smiled. "Your face will make the front page of the Martian Chronicle..."

Marcus didn't respond. He was still baffled by his metaphysical experience. He began to consider what he had seen in that vision. The most disturbing thing was the news from his wife that

Jeff and his son were about to leave for Titan. That was the ultimate confirmation that he had somehow seen into the future...

"Jeff, listen to me. Charlotte told me that you are leaving for Titan tomorrow with your son, is that correct?"

"Yes, I know it's all of a sudden, but Douglas won two free tickets. How could I refuse? Free spaceflights, free accommodation, you can't turn that down." He paused raising his eyebrows to mark his point. "Boy I'm looking forward to it....The spacecraft responsible for our trip is newly designed, powered by ion engines. Anyway, I've cleared it with the wife. Aurora's happy for us to go. I can't wait... What an experience it will be, visiting the largest moon of Saturn...the second largest natural satellite in the solar system. I read that it was once famous for its rivers of liquid methane, and its economy is flourishing you know, as a result of the mass sale of hydrogen mined from the atmosphere." He rubbed his jaw reflectively. "I'm really looking forward to taking pictures of Saturn from the side of Titan's surface that constantly

THE MARS TIME-PROJECT

faces the ringed planet. Did you know that Titan orbits Saturn once every 15 days and 22 hours?"

Marcus stumbled out of the bed with a sense of urgency.

"Hold on Jeff....Listen to me, I know that this might sound bizarre..." He paused for breath and contemplated his words carefully. His eyes moved from left to right. "I had a vision of you and your son leaving for Titan way before I knew you were actually going. In my vision, your ship exploded violently in outer space..."

Jeff stood there silently, eyes wide and mystified...

"Jeff it wasn't a dream..."

"Wait a second, what are you telling me..."

"What I'm telling you is this..." His eyebrows lifted and his strong, cultivated voice rolled on. "I've experienced a vision of the future... This has to be somehow connected with my journey in time with Quantum Effect."

"I see," replied Jeff, now deeply concerned for his sanity. "So, in essence, you're claiming to be some kind of a prophet now...a fortune teller? Marcus, come on my friend..."

"Listen to me! I had a vision... and it's one you need to consider, as it directly affects you and your son. Jeff, you have known me for many years, I've never been into astrology or palm-reading, but I'm telling you, somehow I've experienced a vision of the future. Something must have happened in that time-machine. Some kind of metaphysical doorway has opened within my mind, esoteric power, there's no explanation otherwise...Strict logic will tell you that."

"So, you are predicting my death and the death of my son?"

"This isn't a theoretical prediction it was a vision of an event that will take place. Of course, if you listen to me you can avoid it and cheat both death and time."

THE MARS TIME-PROJECT

"Well surely you need to relay this to the spaceport officials for the sake of all the other lives...no?"

"Yes, give me your spaceflight number..."

"Marcus my friend they will laugh at you. What proof can you give them? They will take you for insane."

"I can't give them any proof...this can't be measured in any way to see whether or not it's true. There is no scientific method involved here. This can't be placed under a microscope and analysed. This is a metaphysical experience...I've seen into the future and that must be accepted blindly regardless of how bizarre it sounds."

"Marcus..." Jeff paused and cleared his throat..."I think the stress of your experience with Quantum Effect has somehow affected your mind. It's almost as if you're suffering from some type of situational psychosis. After all, your brain was subjected to an enormous amount of strain given the nature of the task, not to mention the implantation of the time recall device and its removal."

"I tell you that I knew about your trip to Titan before my wife told me. That doesn't bother you? How do you explain that? This has nothing to do with stress, psychosis, and strain. It happened I tell you."

"Marcus, in that case, it was nothing other than a weird unexplainable dream... that I'm sure of, regardless of your apparent foreknowledge of my trip to Titan. What you need to do is rest and focus on a new life. You've received a handsome payment for your brave historic venture...Your name is echoing all over Mars and the solar system as the first man to journey three hundred years into the future. If you come out with this, you'll be taken as a mad man. Trust me let it go my friend..."

Marcus, resigned to the fact that his friend wasn't going to believe him, sat on the bed with defeat etched into his eyes. He decided not to push any further. Could it have been a bizarre freakish dream? he suddenly thought, his chain of reasoning slightly altered. Further doubts started plaguing him. A tug of war was taking place within the depths of his mind. He glanced quickly about the room and then said as a sheepish final attempt, "What if I'm right?"

Jeff cut him short and replied, "Highly improbable Marcus. I'll see you soon. As soon as I return from Titan, we'll get in touch…"

The next day Marcus was in a restaurant, trying to relax, his eyes picking out individuals at random. It was a claustrophobic atmosphere. Sitting there he contemplated the gourmet food spread before him. He had ordered the early Martian meal with particular care, thinking deeply about his experience. He finally decided to brush it aside, even though it pulsed relentlessly, deep within the confines of his mind. He licked his lips, and the corner of his mouth twitched. Across the large tele-set which hung high, a news broadcast flashed into life… a weather warning: It read… *Sandstorm gusts reaching 155 kilometres per hour expected in the northern city of New Oslo tomorrow…* Then, suddenly, a figure detached itself from a group of diners, holding onto a small electric guitar. It was a mutant with protruding upper teeth and an abnormally large skull with an ape-like jaw. His head was hairless. He walked over to Marcus with no malicious intent and sat before him.

"I knew I recognised you. Marcus Harlan, the first man to journey ahead in time," he said his words tumbling out in a rasping torrent. "You've made history, Sir. Your face has appeared all over the papers and the news. You're as important as the robot vehicles that helped terra-form this planet..."

Marcus gave a quick smile of acknowledgement as he chewed on a piece of meat. A mutant, he thought. Possibilities of a misunderstanding were great. However, he embraced the mutant's kindness. He broke his stare and spoke.

"Thank you..." he muttered gallantly.

"This is the age of machinery, advanced machinery... I mean a time-machine. The technicians behind its construction have brains beyond," the mutant said. "The technology that's available today is mind blowing; new inventions every day. Who knows, in time, even biological miniaturization could be possible...I like the thought of that. Just imagine a human shrunk to the size of an insect in order to perform a particular task."

"Biological miniaturization is scientifically impossible my friend. You can't miniaturize atoms. Not to mention that even if you could, there would not be enough atoms in their tiny brains to make the brain complex enough to be a human brain."

The mutant shrugged and said, "Well it was a pleasure meeting you Mr Harlan...all the best."

He stood up and made his way back to the group.... Marcus' gaze instantly returned to the tele-set. From where he was sitting, he had a commanding view. The flickering images demanded his attention. A documentary about how Mars was terraformed had just commenced. It reminded him in a flash that the weak gravitational field of the planet meant that the atmosphere was in danger of being lost to outer space. It had to be constantly replenished and kept warm. He focused on the screen where a large ship was pictured making its way to the red planet. Then it showed images of the Mars descent vehicle. It was built for one purpose... to get the first brave humans from Mars orbit to the surface, safely, in a controlled fashion. He could see the parachutes attached to the Mars descent vehicle. He could also see some light thrusters. The picture changed to show all the supply vessels scattered across the red, barren surface. All supplies for surface operations had been deposited in advance. This was duly achieved via unmanned missions prior to the attempt. He could now see a Professor Antoine Lavoisier talking about the whole process. Subtitles made up for the lack of sound in the chaos of the restaurant. Professor Lavoisier said: *'piloting the Mars descent vehicle down to the surface would have been an uncomfortable experience. The first part of this nail-biting experience was to descend from the mother spacecraft, the main ship. In order for the Mars descent vehicle to fall properly, they would have had to decelerate their orbital velocity. Once they hit the atmosphere at a speed of 28,000 kph they would have encountered some turbulence, a bumpy descent to the surface to say the least. Thrusters would have been used in order to slow descent and control their lateral motion.'* The image of the Professor talking faded... Then, the most important, vital piece of the

THE MARS TIME-PROJECT

advance supplies came into sharp view... the Mars ascent vehicle, in effect mini spaceship. It was used for one reason alone... getting back to the main spaceship once everything was complete. The Mars ascent vehicle made its own fuel. This was achieved with help from the Martian atmosphere. It was a fairly simple process. The first step was to collect CO_2 and store it in a high-pressure vessel. Next he could see the brave men in their space suits entering the Mars descent vehicle... He turned his head away from the tele-set and began thinking about his friend and his son. He hoped that all would be well...Time would tell.

Marcus entered his hut at precisely four o'clock. As he closed the front door, he walked towards the kitchen increasing in pace. His wife stood beside the sink. Her face was blotchy and red, and her eyes were filled with tears. Instant panic besieged him.

"What's wrong, tell me?"

"Marcus..." she croaked in a weak, damp whisper. "Jeff and his son and everyone on board spaceflight 101 to Titan are dead. The spaceship blew up as it entered free space. All two-hundred wiped out... Investigators are baffled as to why this happened... a technical malfunction most likely the cause." She paused, and the anguish was clearly manifested across her face. "I feel so sorry for Aurora... She must be completed devastated losing both her husband and son. I should really try and contact her, but what does one say in a moment like this? It's been a while since I saw her, we were so close..."

Marcus' eyes widened with terror. An overwhelming feeling of guilt cut through him like a knife. He slumped at the kitchen table. He was numb. No tears...His heart stopped then pounded again.... He had to remain calm and confront the situation.

"Charlotte, I didn't tell you this, but yesterday in the bedroom, I had a vision of this exact event taking place. The vision then ceased, and a few seconds later you came into the bedroom and told me that

THE MARS TIME-PROJECT

Jeff was here, and that he wanted to see me. You then informed me of his trip." Marcus began to sweat and realized he was trembling.

"What are you saying Marcus?" She peered anxiously at him.

Unsure how to continue, he cleared his throat to break the silence. Then his dominant personality took charge. He said, "I had a vision of the spacecraft exploding in outer space, Charlotte. All perished. In fact, I'll give you more detail. In the vision I saw Jeff and his son at the spaceport. Next I could see the ship leaving Mars. Next I could see all the passengers sitting in the ship including Jeff and his son Douglas. Then the two pilots...the control-room. Destruction then followed. The ship blew apart..."

Charlotte stood there in shock, her jaw hanging in disbelief.

"I warned Jeff. I told him about my experience when he came upstairs to see me. He totally dismissed it. He said it was a stress induced occurrence, at best, a weird unexplainable dream. In turn I had no choice but to let it go, even though deep down I feared the worse. I've not had any further visions... however it appears that I've somehow developed powers to see into the future...There's no mathematics involved here. This is pure metaphysics... supernatural!"

"I can't believe what I'm hearing. How...?"

"Charlotte, it's true. It happened...you've got to be a believer. My journey through the fourth dimension has somehow opened a doorway within my mind. There's no scientific way to explain it... it belongs to the paranormal realm. I witnessed the deaths of all on board prior to it happening...period!"

He began to plough back through his thoughts, his metaphysical experience, moving his lips slightly in subconscious vocalization. Charlotte sat beside him, searching his face closely for any hint that this was an ill-conceived joke. Every ragged nerve in her body screamed for release. First there had been the anxiety that accompanied the whole time-travel project and now this! She was lost for words,

THE MARS TIME-PROJECT

confused, yet something within told her that what he was saying was true, even though it seemed totally bizarre... She leaned in and hugged him tightly.

Later that night, Marcus sat alone in the living room, the tele-set playing on low volume. Charlotte was curled up in bed, in distressed mode. He sat on the comfy red sofa overwhelmed with a feeling of guilt. His eyes moved to and fro, gazing vacantly at the paintings that were fixed to the pale blue walls. Perhaps he could have prevented it had he pressed harder, he thought. He tried to clear his mind and focused on the tele-set. A documentary had started... Quantum Chromodynamics – Theoretical physics. His mind began to work, needing the distraction... Quantum chromodynamics, the theory of the strong interaction between quarks and gluons, the fundamental particles that make up composite hadrons such as the proton, neutron and pion, he thought... For a brief flicker of a moment he began to think back to his days at school. He remembered his physics teacher, a short skinny man saying to the class: *'All life started as a result of an imperfection at an atomic level...order out of chaos. The atom that lacks an electron, the unstable atom, looks to merge with another atom to make up for its missing electron. This is known as covalent bonding. This whole process only occurs due to a deficient number of orbiting electrons. As a result, life begins... atoms inter-combine and form very complex molecules, proteins, DNA, etc. The whole evolutionary process begins. With regard to the so-called eight-electron, stable, perfect atom...well it's useless. Although considered perfect, the stable atom does nothing. This proves that there is no such thing as perfection. Perfection doesn't exist. It's only a construct of the mind...'* The images and words faded. He picked up the small silver remote and switched channels. Again, another documentary was in full flow. A heavily bearded professor appeared on the screen, a Professor Nickolaus A. Watterson saying: *'Frequency cures cancer. Every organ within the body resonates at a certain frequency including a tumour. By using a frequency that is similar to the frequency of cancer cells (reverse polarity) tumours are destroyed...Thankfully we have the cure...'* Marcus suddenly felt dizzy. His head spun. He stood up. Then he fell to his knees holding his stomach as if hit by a bolt of lightning... He lay across the floor, his eyes wide as if he were dead.

He attempted to move but couldn't. Then images sparkled into being in the same form as before...an oscillating haze, the images, clear and sharp. He could see a gang of anti-religious mutants planting a series of bombs at a Hindu convention. They gradually faded out and resolved to show the building totally demolished...all lives taken...total destruction! As a brutal fear set in, he started to shake violently. His eyes grew heavy. He closed them and slowly fell into unconsciousness...

As the dim early morning sun rose, Marcus awoke drenched in sweat. For a moment he couldn't move, all memory lost. But mental vitally and movement were soon restored in a prompt flash. His mind was brilliantly lit by the vision he'd had. Instantly he rose from the floor and stood. He could hear footsteps. Charlotte walked in yawning...

"Charlotte it happened again..."

"What! Marcus...?"

"A vision of the future..."

ANTHONY FUCILLA

"What?"

He paced towards her, held her and said, "In my vision I saw a gang of anti-religious mutants planting a series of bombs at a Hindu convention."

"Where...?"

"That I don't know, but what I do know is everyone was killed!"

"Marcus, you're scaring me?"

"Listen... it happened, just like before. We've got to stop it!"

"But there are hundreds of religious Hindu conventions here on Mars that take place weekly, spread all over the planet."

Marcus turned away from her and walked towards the window gazing out into the distance and said, "If only I knew the City... the exact location of this convention, I could stop it. Perhaps I should inform the government, the Mars-police patrol!"

"And what will you tell them? As you said, you don't know the exact location!"

He turned and faced her...

"They won't take you seriously Marcus...I'm sorry, but there's nothing you can do."

"So, what are you saying?" he countered. "I have a responsibility Charlotte."

Suddenly across the tele-set the morning hourly news show commenced. Marcus sprang over and increased the volume. The time was displayed at the bottom of the screen. It read 11:00am. Both Marcus and Charlotte waited with an eerie expectancy. The female news reporter then said: *Breaking news... one-hundred and fifty people have tragically lost their lives at a Hindu convention in New Oslo. The building blew up just under twenty minutes ago. A gang of anti-religious mutants are suspected of having planted a series of bombs....The Hindus are most famous for their journeys into the mountains, where they gather and meditate for days...The Galaxius Mons mountain range and Olympus Mons, one of the tallest mountains in the solar-system, are their favourite spots for spiritual enlightenment...'*

Marcus jabbed at the cut-off button shutting down the tele-set. The screen slowly faded to black. Charlotte stood there completely shocked.

Marcus grabbed her left arm and said, "Charlotte, now you know that I have powers to see into the future and I don't see any reason why these visions will stop...more will follow..."

Charlotte went rigid with total dismay. After a few seconds of intense contemplation, she shrugged him off and walked over to the sofa where she sat chewing her lip. She tried to repress the feeling of dread that possessed her. A short silence followed...

"Charlotte," he snapped, trying to shake her out of herself, his heart pounding. He hesitated, "I've got to go to Quantum Effect and explain what has been happening to me."

"But what will they do?"

"I don't know exactly."

"But Marcus..."

"Listen Charlotte..." He paused and rubbed his forehead. "I need to go there and talk to them. This is all happening as a result of my journey in time, don't you see? It's vital that I go. They need to know about these visions...visions of the future. I'm going up-stairs now to change and freshen up...then I'm leaving."

Marcus briskly left the room and made his way up the stairs, two at a time. Charlotte would have to deal with this as best she could. He did not have time to comfort her now. As he entered the bedroom countless thoughts plagued his now fatigued, perturbed mind. He went to open the cupboard door, but his hand froze. Panic engulfed him. He moved towards the bed staggering like a drunken man and collapsed. He tried to move his lips in a desperate plea, to cry out, but failed. He was numb all over. Then suddenly, another vision came... The world he knew faded... He saw images of Planet Earth. An oscillating haze, yet clear, sharp, just as before. The images continued as he lay lifeless on the bed, arms flung aside. It was as if he were suspended in outer space just watching the giant blue sphere of Earth rotate brilliantly in the star-filled silence. Next he could see a giant city. It came all of a sudden. He saw a sign. It read... *'Welcome to the city of Osaka.'* It was Japan. The people of Mars were well informed about the cities of Earth. He could see people roaming in energetic patterns; hover-cars sweeping across the skies, surface vehicles speeding across the well-structured organised roads. The streets glinted as if stars had fallen to the ground. Then a horrific quake came. The earthquake was so powerful that instant death and destruction followed... a soup of utter chaos and devastation... In a flash the vision had gone. Marcus lay on the bed his heart beating fast... He closed his eyes. He knew that the news of this horrific quake would soon come. Rapidly he rose from the bed, dashed out of the room, and made his way down the stairs. As he entered the living room, Charlotte was still sitting on the sofa in a state of obvious distress and concern...

"Marcus, I thought you were going to get changed and freshen up?"

THE MARS TIME-PROJECT

"Charlotte please, it happened again...!"

"What? You mean another vision? Upstairs?"

He didn't respond, but the look in his pain-filled eyes confirmed it with dreadful clarity.

"What did you see?"

"I saw a city being destroyed as a result of seismic activity, plate tectonics, an Earthquake!"

"Where...?"

"Planet Earth...the city of Osaka in Japan."

He jabbed at the activation button. The tele-set instantly came to life. The Mars news channel was visible. He walked over to the sofa and sat stiffly beside Charlotte.

"I'm not moving from here until the news filters through...and believe me, it will!"

He rubbed his eyes and gazed towards the tele-set with anticipation. An hour swept by as they both sat in stunned silence...To them it was as if minutes had passed; time altering its properties in the fear of the moment. Then it came...A black haired, sharp-eyed female news reporter said... *'Breaking news from Planet Earth: The city of Osaka Japan was hit by a severe Earthquake five minutes ago. Thousands die...'*

Marcus leapt off the sofa shutting the tele-set with the remote in hand. He then tossed it toward the sofa and there it lay.

"That's it! I'm leaving now Charlotte. I'm going Quantum Effect..."

Charlotte was gripped with horror. Her eyes were wide and perplexed... "Marcus I can't believe what is happening..."

"Charlotte, I know it's hard to take, but this has become a burning reality. More visions are bound to follow."

He paused, turned, and made his way for the door...

THE MARS TIME-PROJECT

Marcus entered the dome...Quantum Effect. Rushing over to the familiar receptionist, the young brunette, he said in a somewhat jerky manner, "I need to see Professor Clarkson or Molloy urgently."

The receptionist instantly saw that something wasn't quite right.

"Why Mr Harlan! Are you okay?" Her green eyes fluttered as she awaited his reply. She smiled. Her teeth sparkled white.

He pushed out his chest, focused and said. "It's important that I speak to them now."

"Professor Paul Molloy is in the building somewhere... however Professor Clarkson is not here today."

"Molloy will be fine," he said sharply.

The receptionist fiddled with the small slick computer before her and said, "I've just sent a message through. He's responded instantly and will be with you shortly Mr Harlan."

Within a few minutes, Molloy came walking over with purpose, rubbing his thick grey moustache, which had been neatly trimmed for the cameras. He halted a meter away. His cold blue eyes lit up and he said, "Mr Harlan, what a pleasant surprise to see the man of the hour who has made Martian history. What brings you back here?"

"What happened to me in that time-chamber was as a result of your brilliance Professor, but thank you all the same..."

Molloy smiled. Almost a cheeky smile....

"So, Mr Harlan, what can I do for you?"

"Can we speak in private please?"

Molloy pointed politely towards a silver door. It stood at the far end of the hall...

"After you Mr Harlan..."

Within minutes both Marcus and Molloy were seated in a brilliantly lit room, eyes nailed together. It was quite bare. Pale walls surrounded them.

"So, Mr Harlan, what can I help you with...?"

Molloy's partially bald head glistened as he sat there calm and sharp eyed. Seconds of dead silence passed...

"Professor Molloy, since my journey in time I've started having visions...so far, three."

Molloy's eyes widened... He raised a brow with a measure of authority and said, "Visions, what visions?"

"Visions of three horrific disasters... They all took place."

"What did you see?" asked Molloy, his face now a manifestation of deep intrigue.

"In my first vision I saw my friend and his son at the Mars spaceport. They were leaving Mars and heading to Titan. Next I could see the ship leaving Mars. I then saw all the passengers sitting in the ship...the two pilots...the control-room. Destruction followed in outer space. The ship blew apart...a devastating explosion..."

"Yes, I heard about this disaster. Do you mean to tell me that you knew that this was going to happen before it actually did?"

"Yes, that's exactly what I'm saying..."

"So why didn't you warn your friend? Why didn't you contact the Mars spaceport and tell them what you had experienced?"

"I told my friend Jeff. He dismissed it. He believed it was a stress induced experience... my journey in time, the enormous amount of strain given the nature of the task, not to mention the implantation of the time recall device and its removal. He then said towards the end of our discussion that it could have been a weird unexplainable dream... In short, he persuaded me to let it go, otherwise I would have contacted the Mars spaceport. Doubts then started to form in my mind...I never followed it up but should have." Marcus paused and rubbed his jaw. "You don't seem surprised by all of this, Professor."

"How could I be Mr Harlan? I'm a scientist. I built the time-chamber along with Professor Clarkson and a few other elite scientists. Why would this surprise me? Here at Quantum effect you had the ultimate vision of the future... three hundred Martian years into the future, so from a logical perspective, why would I be surprised?"

"No time machine involved here Professor..."

"Yes indeed..."

"So, explain..."

"Mr Harlan, what you encountered lies within the realms of pure metaphysics. I have no explanation. Whatever the case, something must have happened to you in the time-chamber. You have obviously developed a paranormal ability, no question. Some kind of doorway has opened up within the deepest regions of your brain. Remember Mr Harlan, a human being is a very complicated electro chemical physical mechanism with the mind and the personality seated in the brain's operations... The mind is the most complex thing in our universe, a spatial temporal construct, a network of approximately one hundred billion neurons. Tell me about the other two visions..."

"In my second vision which occurred last night, I saw the destruction of a building. Many lives were lost. It was the Hindu convention in New Oslo, although during the vision I was unsure of the exact location. This horrific event then took place today, early morning. It was confirmed on the news."

"Yes, I heard about it, this morning. A gang of anti-religious mutants are suspected of having planted a series of bombs....one-hundred and fifty people died. And your third vision...?"

"Vision three came today. It was the quake on planet Earth in the city of Osaka, Japan...I saw its destruction, a ghastly sight. Just over an hour later it was confirmed on the news...After that I made my way here."

"This I've yet to hear of..."

Marcus promptly interjected, "Professor," he muttered, "please, can you help me then?"

"Mr Harlan I'm absolutely fascinated by this paranormal ability that you have obviously acquired as a result of your journey in time here at Quantum Effect but what do you mean by help? I can't stop these visions Mr Harlan, nor can I explain them. As I said, this lies within the realms of the paranormal. However, I can scan your brain with immediate effect."

"What would be the point Professor?"

"Analyse brain activity. I'm not saying that this will shed any light on the matter, but it would be interesting to see what's happening within your brain from a neurological perspective."

Shortly thereafter, Marcus was lying inside a white tube of light. They were in a large room on level two. Across the wall was a large luminous diagram of the human brain. Sections were marked out like a map. It read: Frontal Lobes, Parietal Lobes, Temporal Lobes, Occipital Lobes, Cerebellum and Brain Stem. Suddenly, the scanning process commenced as, with a professional hand, Molloy activated the machine with the turn of a button. He walked over to a large screen and began to study the images produced... His eyes scanned them meticulously...

"Mr Harlan, brain wave function and activity appears completely normal. Remember, inside the mind of a human being, billions of neurons fire, creating waves of electricity. Different states of mind have different wave frequencies..."

Molloy continued to watch with an analytical eye in search of any neurological abnormalities, but nothing appeared.

"If one really considers what we are made of Mr Harlan, one is left in utter astonishment. We are made of tiny particles held together by invisible forces. Everything is made up of energy. The atoms that humans are made of have negatively charged electrons... Anyway, the scan relays no abnormalities whatsoever. Brain activity appears normal..."

He looked on for a time then deactivated the machine... The white metallic tube of light which encased Marcus retracted. He was now free to move. Marcus rubbed his eyes and stood.

"Professor what next...?"

"Mr Harlan, our objective here at Quantum Effect has been achieved brilliantly. You journeyed ahead in time, three hundred years and as a result made history. We brought you back safely and you were rewarded for your bravery. In terms of these visions which appear to be somehow connected to your quantum journey in time, well unfortunately there's nothing more I can do. There's no doubt in my mind that something happened to you during your experience. A metaphysical region of the brain has somehow been activated, a supernatural region of the brain but this is really a matter of metaphysics..."

"So that's it?" snapped Marcus anxiously. "I'm now some kind of Martian Guru I guess, unable to control this paranormal power at work in me. With this acquired gift, if you can even call it that, comes infinite pain and responsibility."

"Yes, Mr Harlan indeed it does," replied Molloy, with little sympathy. "However, I'm fascinated by these visions. Please keep in touch. You are more than welcome to come back here and share...anytime..." And that was it... Marcus was dismissed.

Marcus sat alone in his Martian hut. Charlotte was out. He wondered where she had gone... That thought soon dissipated. He sat absorbed in the silence. It was like the air was charged with static electricity. Thoughts began surging through his mind. What will be next he thought? What will I see...? When will it come? A sudden idea then came to him... He began to wonder whether this 'acquired gift,' would work in terms of predicting future events without the need of a vision. He closed his eyes for a time, but nothing came. He then wondered whether he could predict a number, role a dice, and attain a positive predictive conclusion.

Number three came to mind. From the small cabinet beside him, he produced a leather dice cup and he rolled in grand manner with a backwards twist to his wrist...The dice rolled then promptly stopped, laying there across the small living room table. He looked over. It was number two. Wrong prediction! He tried again. Five he mumbled aloud. He rolled the dice this time without the aid of the leather dice cup. He looked over. It was number six. Again, he was wrong. No point continuing, he thought. Based on the laws of probability and statistics he would eventually get it right... This was a mathematical certainty. He briskly concluded that beyond his visions he was without paranormal power... Then impulsively, he snapped on the tele-set and gazed towards the screen dreamily... A documentary played away about how Mars was Terraformed and how humans would change over time in an evolutionary way... He sat there trying to forget the agony of his predicament and watched for a time...He needed a distraction in order to calm his troubled mind... He could see Mars in the early days, prior to it being colonised. The surface of the planet was scared by huge geological features, craters, cannons, and volcanoes. He then began to think what the ancients must have thought of it as they studied it and gazed at it in the night sky from Earth... Its redness and fluctuating intensity must have stood out as it wandered through the stars, he thought. The early telescopes must have satisfied many great minds he concluded, aiding them with images never seen by the human eye. He looked on... He could now see images of the two moons of Mars with which he was well familiar, Phobos and Deimos. He could now see the first brave men that were selected, via the selection committee, for the first journey. Guinea-pigs, he thought. What were the criteria for such selection, he wondered? Brave, intelligent men that lacked fear...that lacked a thalamic impulse, and were overtaken by scientific curiosity, blinded by it in fact! Marcus thought on.... They were leaving behind everything that they had known...all reality as they knew it. Yet at the same time, they would have to remain composed for the historic mission and adapt accordingly...Until that point, the beauty of Mars had existed only in the human mind. That soon changed...! He chuckled! Without the presence of man, it was nothing other than a vast collection of atoms...Mars, the Red planet! A speck of matter within the cosmos, with constant albedo changes! The beauty of the universe, the very meaning of it is contained within the sphere of intelligent life...consciousness. Man is the consciousness of the universe! The consciousness of the universe had to be expanded beyond earth for it to continue. The consciousness of the universe had to be taken to other frontiers for it to last...and indeed it did!

Now...for the men he thought... These men specialised in robotics, engineering, medicine, psychiatry, psychology, scientists...biologists, astrophysicists, geologists, architects and more he concluded. He could now see the men living at the North Pole, a cold harsh environment, somewhat similar to what was to come. All part of the training... He could see the men running through simulations of the various tasks they would be performing on the spaceship. Next he could see a spaceship orbiting earth at 28,000 km per hour. Rockets fired powerfully, they accelerated violently. At 40,000 km per hour the burn ended...the ship was free...Mars its destination. It would be a nine-month voyage... All the men on board floated weightlessly around the room with mixed, confused emotions.

Computers worked away, displaying vital bits of information across screens. Then from the control console, the pilots gave the orders to fire lateral control rockets; the ship began to spin. All the men on board sunk to the floor. They stood handsomely in a pseudo gravity of .38g. Due to the pull, balance was achieved with relative ease and without pressure...Then Marcus started to think about the subatomic winds they would have encountered in deep space, the deadly cosmic radiation! Sensitive electrical components would have had to be boxed.

He then saw the men on board covering plants. Frozen embryos had to be stored accordingly. He then started to wonder if many had hallucinated, heard voices? A kind of Space psychosis...? It was highly probable he concluded. Shortage of sensory stimuli would be partly responsible. He could now see the men exercising with zeal on the exercise machines on board the ship. The face of Professor Wolfgang Handel, a contemporary Mars astrophysicist then appeared across the screen. He said... *During the expedition, the colonists had to film and broadcast all events that took place on board the ship so that the people of earth could see this historic moment. Most of the activity on the ship was transmitted to Terra so that all the people of Earth could watch in awe and wonder. Robot cameras were responsible for all the footage on board the ship.'* Across the tele-set, the image changed... He could now see the ship approaching Mars. It was about to go into orbit around the Red planet. The screens and the monitors worked away feverishly. The ship hit Mars' thin high atmosphere at 40,000 kilometres per hour. The heavy vibration and low roar within the ship must have been frightful, he concluded. The screens were bursting with a severe pink-orange glow. Compressed air was bouncing off the heat shields and blazed red. Exterior cameras relayed all. Marcus watched on... He could then see the men on board the ship succumbing to returning gravity. Sudden gravity would have caused breathing and vision problems, he thought. The same astrophysicist, Professor Wolfgang Handel, then appeared on the screen and said, *'The ship would have moved through the thin air at a speed and height calculated to put them into what is called transitional flow.'* Aero-dynamists were responsible for the term transitional flow, Marcus instantly concluded. He had heard of the term before. The brilliance of Man was capable of manipulating matter right down to a molecular level, he thought. The astrophysicist then went on to say... *'Transitional flow is a state between free molecular flow and continuum flow...'* He went on... *'Had they hit a high-pressure cell in the atmosphere, the heat, vibration, or G-forces produced could have caused machinery and mechanisms to break within the ship. All men on board could have perished horribly too. As it turned out, fate was on their side...even the Martian stratospheric weather was stable...The Gods were with them... Special sensors revealed with precise clarity that the dominant heat shield had reached a scorching 601 degrees Kelvin. After that, the turbulence on board the ship came to a halt. They had hopped out of the Martian atmosphere and the ship slowed down by approximately 19,000 kilometres per hour. The sensor now indicated that the heat shield had risen to almost its maximum tolerance level. The sensor relayed the temperature with starling accuracy. It had reached 712 degrees Kelvin. All on board would have floated with merry weightlessness again. After approximately half an earth day, their new course led them to a periapsis 34,000 kilometres from the Red planet. Main rockets were then fired. This would have increased their velocity by approximately 100 kilometres per hour. As a result of this, they were pulled almost magnetically towards Mars, closer to the Red Planet, within 500 kilometres of the surface...Martian orbit!...'* Marcus sat totally absorbed by what he was hearing and viewing. The astrophysicist then said... *'Each elliptical orbit of the Red planet took around a day. High-Tec, complex computers were in total control of all...algorithms, computer logic, decision algorithms!'*

Marcus could now see the chaotic Martian volcanoes in all their glory, the giant eye of Mars, the infinite dunes, and sandy orange-red rugged craters scattered everywhere across the tele-set. Next the astrophysicist Professor Wolfgang Handel said, *'The stamina, and sheer will of man to conquer the solar system, the stars and beyond, was the main ingredient as to why Mars was terraformed successfully...'* Next, drained of emotion, he could see men dressed in their space suits, moving through the ship. Some of the men were sitting in the landing vehicle, belted in. The descent to Mars was coming... Rockets fired, and the landing vehicle drifted away from the ship. Rockets fired again. As a result, they fell towards the planet, hitting the top of the Martian atmosphere. Their single window became a blazing furnace of Martian air.

Marcus now began to think about planet formations. How rocks smashed together in the void of space. Over time planets were formed as a result of gravity, the fundamental force which held the universe of matter within its grip...! Mars itself would have been a bigger planet had it not been for the neighbouring gas giant Jupiter, he suddenly thought. Its immense gravitational field robbed Mars of much of its potential material and mass, as it formed and reached hydrostatic equilibrium. Jupiter had also prevented another planet forming in-between the two because of its strong gravitational field; the asteroid belt, remnants of what could have been. He could now see the northern hemisphere of Mars... It was filled with craters... an old impact basin, a mineral existence! These huge impacts caused severe explosions. Each of these explosions released heat that melted surrounding rock. Elements were broken out of their matrix. Hot gases were produced... liquids...!

THE MARS TIME-PROJECT

Then he could see the first men walking, bouncing on the Red Planet, the winds giving natural co-operation, their boots crunching against the sandy, dark, rusty orange surface, adjusting to the gravity, at ease in their space suits after years of training. They looked up into the pink-orange sky. History was made! He could now see the first men entering their Martian habitats bunching around computer terminals. They also ate and drank within, gazing out of the windows at the Martian sky, where the seasons were twice as long as earth's and everyday was forty minutes longer. The human biorhythm would now be altered for all time... the chronological evolutionary human time pattern!

He began to think... Life adapts under certain conditions. Organism and environment change together. Life adapts... All it needs is some fuel, some energy, all exploited within the Terran environment, that is, it extracts its needs from the surrounding environment. Some organisms live below the freezing point of water...others above the boiling point. Indeed, life adapts... Some live in high radiation zones or within solid rock...some survive dehydration or without oxygen. It is one great biosphere... he concluded. He started to contemplate the mind, the minds of the colonists... Extroversion, introversion was one of the best studied systems of traits in psychological theory. It was a study of one's personality...He then began to think about extroversion. Extroversion was linked with resting states of low cortical arousal, introversion with high cortical arousal. The whole compilation of extrovert and introvert traits can be linked back to a group of cells in the brain stem known as the ascending reticular activating system. It regulated cortical arousal accordingly.

He could now see that roads had been built, excavation machines at work... He could see cities being built, rovers driving across the Martian desert. The cities grew quickly, filled with people, like fungus over a rock! He could see the orbital mirrors that were used to reduce the planet's Albedo. Greater sunlight absorption was the key in terraforming the planet he thought. Heating the planet and releasing carbon dioxide into the atmosphere created a green-house effect. Over time, the atmosphere was produced. The planet was gaining oxygen fast...! Professor Wolfgang Handel then appeared across the screen again and said, *'Algae breaks down carbon dioxide to make oxygen, and its dark colour helped lower Mars's albedo. This in turn helped Mars trap more of the Sun's heat rather than reflecting it back into space. With regard to turning the red planet blue.... Mars had vast amounts of water frozen as ice, both in its polar caps as well as underground, all the way down to the mid-latitudes. Increasing the temperature and pressure on Mars allowed this ice to melt. In turn lakes and rivers were formed. Furthermore, the first part of the task in terraforming the planet, was to make the atmosphere thicker, to warm the planet and allow water to exist on the surface in liquid form. Furthermore, the Martian atmosphere was thickened by redirecting comets and asteroids to crash into its surface. This in turn released gases and created great heat. Also, huge amounts of greenhouse gases were pumped into the atmosphere heating the planet... the greenhouse effect. Mars in turn was slowly terraformed, however, one thing that terraforming cannot rectify is the problem of radiation as a result of Mars's lack of a magnetic field. This still remains a problem today and is the reason why many Martians get cancer. Thankfully we now have the cure. However, an elite team of scientists here on Mars, are planning to launch a giant magnetic shield into space to protect Mars from solar winds. A powerful-enough magnetic shield launched into space could serve as a replacement for Mars's own lost magnetosphere... The giant magnetic shield will eliminate many of the solar wind erosion processes that occur with the planet's ionosphere and upper atmosphere. If the solar wind were counteracted by the magnetic shield, Mars's atmospheric losses would stop, and the atmosphere would regain as much as half the atmospheric pressure of Earth in a matter of years. The early colonists lived in large shielded habitats to protect them from harmful radiation. They would also have taken time to adapt to Mars's gravity. Mars's gravity is only 38 per cent of Earth's....'*

Next, across the screen, Marcus saw the sun set. He could hear the voice of Professor Wolfgang Handel still chirping away, but he dismissed it. He looked on.... The long twilight slowly ran its course, while there was still a dark purple twilight suffusing the hazy air. His eyes were fixed on the screen...Suddenly he heard the door, his mind spiralling off from the complexities that flashed across the screen. His wife briskly walked into the living room with Aurora...Jeff's wife. He was surprised by her unexpected presence. Sudden guilt besieged him. She was a tall lady, slightly plump, with long red hair, and crystal blue eyes.

THE MARS TIME-PROJECT

Charlotte said, "Marcus, when you left, I decided to go to town. I then unexpectedly met Aurora. She desperately wanted to see you..."

"Marcus," Aurora mumbled somewhat brokenly. "I came back from up north as soon as I heard the dreadful news..." She sat beside him, and her eyes lit with tears... "Why," she said in a soft voice. "Why Jeff and my son...?"

He gazed over at Charlotte, a private look. He registered instantly that she had said nothing about the vision. A secret it would remain, he thought. It would be pointless to mention it to her. It would make matters only worse. He'd be placed in a very difficult, uncomfortable situation, which would demand a deep explanation...deep clarity. Jeff and Douglas were gone. Nothing would change that rigid, morbid fact.

"Aurora I'm deeply sorry," he said meekly, his face filled with bitter sadness. It was registered in his eyes.

"Charlotte tells me that he came here to see you the day before his departure..."

"Yes, correct..." he replied. An overwhelming feeling of guilt hit him like a thunder bolt.

"Aurora, I know it's difficult, but you must accept what has happened. Everything is predestined, written in the stars. What is meant to be...will be. We can't fight that. It's a universal principle. I know it's difficult, but you must be strong... We will help you through Aurora. We are here for you."

He rubbed her head, smiled, then stood up abruptly.

"Charlotte, I need to go out for a while. I won't be long."

"Where are you going now?"

"That's not important at present..." He paused in thought. "Aurora, stay here overnight with us. Once I'm back we will talk more. I won't be long..."

THE MARS TIME-PROJECT

Marcus entered a small neat building located downtown. He swung the large glass door open and walked up to the receptionist with steadfast feet and said, "I need to see one of your psychiatrists."

The tall, light-haired, Teutonic-looking receptionist immediately recognised him...

"You're Marcus Harlan aren't you... You're the first man to have journeyed ahead in time. It's an honour to meet you Sir...I'm Brenda."

She stretched out her thin bony hand, and they shook. The rich aroma of perfume suddenly filled his nostrils. Marcus smiled. It was a forced smile, and the look in his troubled eyes suggested so.

"We only operate via pre-booked appointment, however, given that I am standing before a man who has made Martian history," she paused in admiration, playing with her exquisitely tapered fingers. "I think I might just get you a squeeze in with one of our psychiatrists. Wait here Mr Harlan."

She walked away rapidly, disappearing around a corner. He rubbed his eyes in anticipation, wondering, thinking about what would be. Moments later, she came walking over, accompanied by a middle-aged man, dressed in a suave grey Martian suit. From the way he walked, and from the gleam in his eyes, Marcus knew that he wasn't a native, his eyes and his motion so distinct. Judging by his complexion and features he was of Arab extraction. An Arab, an Earthling he thought...It had to be.

"Mr Harlan, this is Dr Madani..." She smiled and her white teeth flashed. "I'll leave you both to it..."

"Mr Harlan, how nice to meet you Sir... I'm standing in front of one of the great Martian pioneers...perhaps the greatest pioneer ever in the solar-system in fact...A quantum journey in time...simply amazing."

"Thank you," he replied. "Tell me Dr, you're not a native Martian, are you?"

"You are very perceptive. The first to notice... I'm actually from planet Earth. I was born in Saudi Arabia but moved to the USA with my parents when I was only two years old. I grew up in the States, but I hold onto my Arab roots and heritage. Regardless, I've been here twenty Earth years, which equates to ten Martian years. My wife and I fancied a change, not to mention that I get paid very well here on Mars." He paused gazing deeply into Marcus's eyes. "So, Mr Harlan, how can I help you?"

"Doctor, I need to speak to you concerning a certain matter. A serious matter..."

"Well as Brenda mentioned, we only operate via pre-booked appointment, however, I can spare an hour for you Sir."

"What's the fee?"

"Well my fees are rather high, but I'll give it a pass this time Mr Harlan... Please follow me..."

They were now sitting in an office. It was unusually warm. A bland looking clock ticking away the Martian seconds hung on the wall facing him. It read three-thirty pm. Just below the clock and fixed to the wall was a glass-framed collection of insects which had been collected and brought to Mars from Earth. A wide variety indeed, he thought as he gazed across. They were dead of course. At the far side of the room, stood a large statue... It was a white sculptured statue of an old Greek philosopher from Earth... Protagoras.

"Well Mr Harlan I'm not a psychic, but basic logic tells me that your journey in time has somehow affected your mental well-being. I'm not surprised given the task you took on. Am I correct?"

"Yes," he replied. "Something has happened to me, ever since my return to natural time."

"What exactly...?" He rested his elbows against the table and pressed his hands together in anticipation.

"I can see into the future."

"I'm sorry! What do you mean?" The doctors' eyes grew wide...

"Exactly that..."

"Do you mean to tell me that you can predict certain events?"

"Not predict. See…"

"In what form do they come? I mean, can you see what is going to happen to me, say in a week from now?"

"It doesn't operate like that Doctor. It's not as if I simply press a button and I suddenly see future events at will. I've had three deadly visions. I didn't cause them…they just happened at random beyond my will. I can't control them. That's basically it…"

The doctor leaned back into his large brown chair, his eyes igniting in wonder.

"How do these visions manifest?"

"It's as if space and time open up before me, and the world that I know fades for a time…then images suddenly appear in an oscillating haze, yet clear, sharp…"

"Tell me about the three visions you've had."

"In short, I witnessed the death of my friend and his son prior to it taking place. A day before in fact... Then, it actually happened. They both perished with many others when their spaceship suddenly exploded. It was a very detailed vision. I saw the ship leaving Mars, all the passengers seated in the ship. Even the two pilots...the control-room. Destruction then followed."

"You mean space-flight 101? I heard about it. Tragic! Mars to Titan journey..."

"Yes, correct."

"If you don't mind me asking Mr Harlan, this might be slightly sensitive, but did you warn your friend and his son? Did you contact the Mars spaceport and tell them what you had experienced?"

A moment of silence fell as they both exchanged piercing eye contact.

"Yes, I told my friend Jeff directly. He wouldn't believe me...said it was a stress induced experience or at best, a weird unexplainable dream that ultimately meant nothing. As for contacting the

Mars spaceport, I didn't. In my second vision, which took place last night, I saw the destruction of a building. Many people died horribly. It was the Hindu convention in New Oslo. Having said this, during the vision itself, I was unsure of the exact location. The exact location was confirmed via the news."

"Yes, I heard about this as well, this morning. And your third vision...?"

"As for vision three, well it came today."

Marcus suddenly paused...his eyes revealing his weariness.

"Well, Mr Harlan..."

"It was...it was the quake on planet earth..."

"I heard the news. The city of Osaka, Japan...thousands died!"

"Yes... I saw its destruction. Then, approximately just over an hour later, it was confirmed on the news..."

"I'm not so surprised about Japan having an earthquake; it is situated in a region of the planet where there is a lot of seismic activity... Japan is very prone to quakes. Regardless, your three visions are truly remarkable..."

"Indeed, they are Doctor..."

"Well, Mr Harlan," said the Doctor professionally, calm and dry. "You've certainly proven that Time is by no means as simple as the relentless onward ticking of the clock. There are, it seems, ripples and discontinuities in time... However, the truth is we still do not understand fully the nature of time. As far as the brain is concerned, time can alter enormously. For example, I can see the whole of creation in one split moment of time in certain mental states. Time is an artefact, the way the brain is constructed. Regardless, your experience at Quantum Effect is no doubt connected to your visions...This lies in the realms of the unexplained...unexplained phenomena, paranormal phenomena. I'm not sure how I can help you. It appears to me that you have acquired a gift from the Gods. You are blessed and cursed. I can only supply medication and counselling here, I'm not really in any position to advise you. This is beyond my expertise. However, I am deeply intrigued by the events."

"More will follow, I'm sure..."

"Perhaps Mr Harlan...! Very likely...I must confess, in all my years of work, I've never encountered anything like this. Don't get me wrong, I have had some bizarre cases, like people claiming to see apparitions, ghosts, which in scientific terms can be defined as ectoplasm. I had one case when I was working on planet Earth, where a man claimed after a brief visit to England, that he had seen Roman soldiers walking out of a wall then vanishing minutes later. I asked myself, what is happening here? Can it be dismissed as a hallucination? But then again, hallucination is a vague and slippery word used to describe something we can't explain or understand. Some scientists claim that if you place the human brain into a very strong magnetic field, you will be able to induce a paranormal experience. An interesting yet weak concept... Other scientists say the human eye is a camera; it forms an image of the outer world on its sensitive screen, the retina, and then transmits it to the brain. Could this system work in reverse they ask? That is, could the brain send images to the eye? The eye then becomes a kind of tele-set screen creating images that don't exist! This could be brought on by depression, sadness or plain expectation. Again, an interesting but weak concept... Another idea is that certain areas are more prone to paranormal phenomena than others, geographically speaking. Many believe that the answer lies in the rock strata beneath...fault lines. These fault lines in some way are generating an energy which is allowing paranormal activity to take place. Minor earth tremors, minor seismic activity could cause many of the poltergeist type effects. Also, inert gas is realised immediately prior to earth tremors. This can take on a luminous glowing form which can appear as an apparition to some. However, the most intriguing possibility is that a form of energy, possibly a sub-microwave level radiation is released by the fault and this in some way interacts with the human neural system, the human brain. This could bring on hallucinations. Again, a weak concept! Regardless, in this particular case, I came to the conclusion that it had actually happened; that is, the man had indeed seen these Roman soldiers...! Thus, my conclusion was that moments of powerful emotion, moments of the past, can be somehow trapped in the rocks, stones, the earth itself, in the surroundings shall we say, to be replayed at a later time. The environment somehow absorbs the energy from living beings that inhabit them. Under certain conditions, that energy, that signal can be replayed at a later date to certain individuals who are open and receptive. In short, energy liberated in a particular point in time is transmitted, expelled into the surrounding material and stored in that material. These subtle energies, a series of vibrational frequencies can then be read out at a later time. Events of the past can be recorded in living matter. This raises the question of whether innate matter has consciousness. Could matter hold impressions of the past? Regardless, in my opinion it implies that, there is survival of mind after death, the first law of thermodynamics will testify to that. In other words, there is a continuation of consciousness after death. Once the brain dies, consciousness continues... this proves that the mind and brain are two separate entities. The mind only works through the brain, operating through it... Anyway, going back to you...In conclusion, there's nothing I can do for you Sir. Nothing I can suggest...This is beyond academic advice, beyond natural science somewhat similar to the example given..."

"Doctor, I understand. This was a desperate attempt. Indeed, what could you or anyone do? I think I need to somehow accept this gift if you like to term it as such... There's no escaping what may follow..."

"Mr Harlan, you can come here anytime, without fee. I'm fascinated beyond belief by these incredible visions. If they occur again, please come see me... We will talk, even though I have no way of advising you about this obviously metaphysical gift that transcends time and space..." He smiled suddenly, his eyes deep, profound. He then said, "I want to leave you with this..."

He revealed a small brown card. Marcus reached over and took it. He started to read the small white print.

"What's this he asked...?"

"It's the address of a very important philosopher. He lives close to here. I think you should go see him at some point. He's a great mind, a man of great knowledge. His name is Democritus. He lives with his one disciple, Solon... both are mutants. When you have the chance, go see him. I've known him several years... He could enlighten you further Mr Harlan..."

Marcus stepped into his hut closing the door behind... Night had fallen. It was dark outside.

"Charlotte," he cried, walking into the kitchen where motion and sound were detected.

He stepped in and said... "Where's Aurora?"

"She left..." She studied him with analytical eyes and said, "Where did you go? You were gone a long time."

He walked over to the kitchen table and sat without reply...

"Well, where did you go Marcus?"

He looked up with glazed eyes and replied, his fatigue evident in his body language, "I went to Masons Psychiatrists..."

"And...?"

"They...or shall I say he," he blasted, "can't help. This is beyond human intervention..."

"What about Quantum Effect? I didn't get the chance to ask you what happened there..."

"Charlotte there's nothing they can do either. Professor Molloy analysed my brain activity. It was normal. Ultimately I'm alone in this..."

Seconds of silence passed...

"Marcus," she said softly. "Please go rest now.... Try to rest your mind. You look so pallid and tired.

The discomforts of the night will be forgotten in the glory of a new day..."

She was looking at him with such solemn sympathy that in a moment all his self-pity vanished. He gazed into her eyes with a symbiotic connection which was like a kiss and cracked his posture...

"Yes, my love, I will... But forget? How can I?" He stood up, his eyes still fixed on her, his mind spinning and twisting with matters beyond human comprehension. "This paranormal gift that I have acquired has taken a lot out of me. More visions will follow Charlotte. And they can manifest anytime..."

She was silent. She rubbed her forehead perplexed. "Marcus," she said tenderly. "Early tomorrow morning I'm going to see Aurora. I've booked an M-cab. I won't stay there too long, I promise you my love. I know you need me by your side... It's just that she's in such a bad way. I fear for her."

"Good idea," he replied, structuring his thinking.

They hugged... a warm, strong intense hug. It was as if both were in search of psychological and physical recharge.

"Okay, I'm going to rest."

He left her presence and made his way for the bedroom upstairs. He lay on the bed, a powerful exhaustion overtaking him. What would he do next? He closed his eyes and fell asleep. Hours drifted by as he dreamt...Meaningless images and faces flashed through his mind during his dream-state...sensorimotor hallucinations!

Then it was morning... a new day, and the sun shone dimly into the room. Marcus slowly awoke to the silence of the hut. His face was hot and slicked with sweat. He knew he was alone. Charlotte had already left. Slowly he started to structure his thinking, his thought patterns. His mind was in a haze. Then suddenly, he was hit with a bolt of force. At least that's how it felt. He was pressed against the bed. Then, that same oscillating haze appeared before him. Images started to form shimmering into existence... He could see a man, a

THE MARS TIME-PROJECT

face standing outside on an open elevated platform giving a speech to a crowd of thousands. In the vision no sound came! The man's eyes were filled with brutal hate and iron determination and he moved his arms with energy. He was dressed in black and his face was somewhat familiar to Marcus in a blurred distorted way...Then, it hit him. It was Larry Schneider, a politician who was gaining great admiration from many throughout Mars; a sharp clever individual, who had a magnetic presence. He was immensely charismatic and was gaining momentum... Images of destruction now flashed before him. He could see Martian wars at play. Riots, death and destruction plagued the planet. Fires roared. Fear and dread gripped the Martian sphere! Lifeless bodies lay scattered throughout. The vision moved on in time; he could see the people of Mars being implanted with Nano-chips... These chips were inserted into the brain, near the temporal lobe. He could then see signals, low frequency radio waves, being sent out from a central base on Mars! This was paranormally displayed to him in the vision... he could actually see electromagnetic radiation. Marcus quickly worked out what was happening almost viscerally! These signals must be able to collect all cephalic data, every thought and emotion via the chips, which had the capacity to store all the necessary neurological information. Total mind control would come he thought! Again, he could see the same man, Mars's future tyrant leader, Larry Schneider dressed in black, sitting in a large room, his face hard yet content with acquired power and control. He drank with glee, sipping at a glass. He could now see another room...the image switching quickly and flashing before him... Larry Schneider appeared standing with an over accentuated confidence and arrogance; an elaborated arrogance. And this time, there was another man present, whose face was hidden by the haze. He sat in a large brown chair dressed in black and his hand was placed on a button, red in colour. He faced a large rectangular screen showing images of Planet Earth. Marcus too could see the beautiful images of Earth displayed vividly across this screen... A jungle appeared steaming with foetid rot, coiled gleaming reptiles moving through the marshes. He could see deadly neurotoxic, cytotoxic and hemotoxic snakes slithering, lions roaring; a vast array of life, a planet saturated in life of countless forms. A desert then appeared dry and arid...various cities, people moving back and forth in a circuitry of chaotic motion...great mountains, the endless miles of oceanic water. Then, for the first time he heard the word, 'fire...' Immediately a button was pressed by the man whose face was still hidden by the blur and haze of the vision. Next he could see a vast array of huge Earth-destroying bombs launching into outer space...deep space. Planet Earth would soon feel the force of the coming Martian missiles. He saw a series of dreadful devastating explosions. Many perished both on land and at sea. Dead clouds of ash drifted into the atmosphere. Blazing fires got their wicked way! Suddenly the vision vanished into oblivion... Marcus lay on the bed as if dead, filled with a cold penetrating dread! His heart constricted, rapidly retrieving its rhythm; metabolic secretions of fear working inside his body. Repressing the thalamic impulses, he recaptured his composure. He did not have time to feel fear.

"A powerful leader is rising to power," he mumbled! "He will take over Mars, creating wars on the Martian sphere and create a mind-controlled society! Planet Earth will also be a victim!"

He pictured the bombs again and the destruction that followed.

"He needs to be stopped at all cost!"

Marcus rose from the bed with a sense of duty. The future of Mars and Earth now lay in his hands. He understood the responsibility and the implications... there was nothing to consider. Kill one man to save the lives of millions...period! Any good moral philosopher will back my decision, he thought. But to the current people of Mars and beyond he would be regarded as a murderer, he concluded! Technically speaking he would be, but it was all for a greater cause unbeknownst to the masses. But that didn't matter. He brushed it all aside. It was pointless pondering on metaphysical ethics. Take out one evil man to save the souls of millions...I'll be remembered as the first man to travel ahead in time, nothing can change that. But I'll also be remembered as a murderer too if I get caught, he thought. His eyes grew wide....

THE MARS TIME-PROJECT

Marcus headed to town at speed... As he entered the busy town centre of Olympus, he saw a crowd slowly gathering. Many were mutants. Then to his utter amazement he saw Larry Schneider with his small group of twisted followers, disciples all dressed in black being interviewed by the Mars News team. This was fate... What were the odds of this occurring directly after his revelation? The mathematical probability of this occurring straight after his vision was beyond numbers, beyond anything! To him, this was a confirmation of his task, as if a greater force were at work, guiding him to his destiny...his mission. He pulled the surface-vehicle over onto a free-bay and parked. He then gazed again towards Larry Schneider almost in disbelief...his jaw hanging, his eyes set upon him like a predator ready to strike! He pulled out the small brown card which was given to him by Dr Madani from his jacket. He read the address which was in small white print. He then vividly recalled the name of the apparent great philosopher... Democritus and his one disciple Solon too... He remembered that they were both mutants. He began to think deeply... Larry Schneider must be eliminated as soon as possible. In order to achieve such a task, I will need help, support, a strategy, words of great wisdom and psychological backing. It's no easy task. If anyone is going to believe me and be able to help, it will be them, especially a deep philosophical mind of that magnitude. The odds were high; mutants in general were prone to believing and accepting the weird and wonderful. Many indulged in mythology and it didn't get any more bizarre than this. However, it was still a risk. They might not believe him, branding him a dangerous mad man. The consequences would then be vast. Regardless, he would have to gamble. He needed numbers, backing... support in order to rid the world of the evil tyrant to come...Marcus stepped out of the surface-vehicle, slapped the door, and walked over towards the crowd. Suddenly their eyes met for a brief second, the eyes of Larry Schneider and his. A cold chill moved through Marcus... His heart began to beat fast, then...

"Hey Marcus, you've made history... the first man to travel ahead in time... I read all about it in the papers. What's it like now you've retired from the detective agency? You are dearly missed there my friend..."

Marcus was startled. It severed his focus. He promptly composed himself as he stood staring at his onetime work colleague Kevin Flynn. He was a tall man, medium build with a bald head. Bits of white hair were visible on the sides of his head and his strong grey moustache stood out boldly.

"Kevin...," he said distractedly. "Good to see you... Yes, my life has changed, changed being the operative word in fact."

"I bet," Kevin replied smiling and waved his arm. "The crowds converge around this seemingly slick upcoming politician Larry Schneider..." He laughed and pointed. "I've no time for politicians. But I must admit this Mr Schneider certainly has a magnetic presence. He's a great orator, great rhetoric. It appears he's slowly rising to power..."

"Yes indeed..." Marcus' mind returned to the vision!

"Are you here in support of him?"

Marcus scowled, and replied, "No... I just came into town for a stroll..."

"I see. Well, I'm sure you've had a few crowds around you. You represent history Marcus. You are a pioneer." He paused rubbing his grey moustache, his eyes gazing towards the ground as he temporarily lost himself in thought. "Anyway, I've got to go now. I was actually on my way to meet a friend... Then I saw the commotion, Schneider and co, and then delightfully you. Hey, it was great seeing you again Marcus... Best wishes..."

He patted him on the back, and departed, disappearing amongst the endless bodies of people. Suddenly, the crowd that surrounded the mars news team and Schneider and his disciples turned and rushed over to Marcus surrounding him like vultures around a carcass.

"Marcus Harlan... the time traveller," they yelled jubilantly with a roar... Within seconds he was surrounded by faces. Voices echoed... Then, Larry Schneider approached, walking at a calculated pace... He squeezed through a few bodies and now faced Marcus. Marcus instantly correlated the images of the vision with the slim pale faced man that stood before him...it had definitely been Larry

THE MARS TIME-PROJECT

Schneider. His heart thudded. His voice was dry... He couldn't believe what was happening. The man he had to kill was now almost face to face with him. What a bizarre sequence of events, he thought but he remained calm....

"We appear to pull the same crowd Marcus Harlan...you a pioneer, the first man to travel ahead in time and me, well let's just say the people like what I have to say. It seems that the same destiny awaits us. I could do with a man like you. Your name is echoing throughout the solar system. You've made history...Martian history as the first great time-traveller. You could do much for me at a political level. We could do great things together...."

A strange feeling overwhelmed Marcus. It cut like a knife. His head spun. Larry with an agile hand, slipped a card from his pocket.

"Here's my card, Marcus. It contains all my contact details. Remember a great destiny awaits us...I feel it."

"Yes, destiny," Marcus mumbled. "There's no doubt!" He took the card with a shaky hand and placed it into his jacket. "I'm sorry but I have other engagements. I've got to go now..."

"Great meeting you... I look forward to hearing from you...soon I hope." Larry smiled.

"Indeed, you will, Mr Schneider..."

Marcus turned and made his way through the awe-struck crowd. He walked up to the surface-vehicle and entered... He then pulled out the card and gazed at it with a feeling of great irony. It will make things a lot easier now, he thought cynically. The man that he was to assassinate was aiding him with contact information, information that could lead to a meeting sometime. He then pulled out the other card and examined it critically. He read the philosophers address and decided it was time!

On the way, Marcus suddenly decided to pull over and get a drink. His throat burned with thirst, and much was on his mind. He needed a bit more time to himself before meeting the great mutant philosopher and his disciple. He saw a small bar and pulled over next to a vegetable delivery van. The windows were fully opened, and he could hear music. The driver sat there nodding and moving his head to the sound, oblivious to what was going on around him. Mind control! Marcus stepped out of the surface-vehicle and made his way to the bar. As he entered, a few people stood around drinking, mouths gaping in idle chat. In the background, music was playing faintly. Hanging overhead in cages, were a variety of mechanical birds; part of the décor. He made his way to the bar. There was a whole selection of alcoholic beverages available. A high-pitched voice caught his attention...the mutant barman. He had severe physical abnormalities; one large eye that was centred above a deformed flat nose.

He said, "What can I get you Sir?"

"A cold Martian beer please..." he replied somewhat distracted, his mind preoccupied with matters of cosmic importance.

"You sure do look familiar Sir," the mutant muttered.

Marcus was keen to avoid the discussion regarding his fame...his journey in time.

"I can't see how. I've never been here before," he replied dismissively.

He smiled weakly and without any further dialogue paid the mutant barman, grabbed the beer and drank greedily. Then, he caught the muffled words of a man conversing with a mutant. His stance and penetrating eyes indicated he was a person with a high intellectual capacity, his thin face alight with the glow of a teacher with a willing pupil. He said to the mutant...

"Jupiter is indeed a mysterious planet...a giant gas planet. A planet formed of hydrogen and helium gases with clouds made up of ammonia ice crystals and the temperature range on the planet varies considerably. The clouds are a freezing -145 degrees Celsius. As you move closer to the core, it reaches scorching temperatures of approximately 35,000 degrees Celsius."

"So, what's Jupiter's atmosphere like then," asked the mutant?

"Jupiter's atmosphere has two prominent visible features... strong winds that form multiple jets of alternating direction between the equator and the poles, and hundreds of very powerful hurricane-like swirling winds known as vortices. The average speed of the jets can be more than 224 miles per hour. Then there's the Great Red Spot; Jupiter's most iconic feature. It's really a monstrous storm consisting of strong swirling winds with a maximum speed of 435 miles per hour."

"The gravity on Jupiter is very strong I hear," commented the mutant, almost overwhelmed by the man's presence.

"Yes, the immense gravitational field of Jupiter is such that it is held responsible for much of the development of nearby celestial bodies, like our planet Mars. The gravitational force of Jupiter stunted the growth and development of Mars, consuming material that would have contributed to its size. It also prevented a new planet forming between these two. This is how the asteroid belt formed. The asteroid belt is nothing other than remnants of a planet that could have been."

"What about Jupiter's magnetic field?" the mutant then asked with great curiosity. His voice was hoarse.

"The magnetic field of Jupiter is 20,000 times stronger than Planet Earth's. It contains a huge number of charged particles that contribute to giant auroras at its north and south poles. The tail of Jupiter's magnetosphere stretches more than one billion kilometres away from the Sun."

An astronomical discussion at play, Marcus thought dismissively. He had no time for that.... He then gazed around absently for a time, everything passing in a blur. He hoped the few people that occupied the bar wouldn't recognize him; he was in no mood for praise or discussion. Then he noticed two females looking him over, almost calculating. They

THE MARS TIME-PROJECT

whispered to each other. They've probably recognized the time traveller, he thought to himself. Then a few other people began to turn and stare inquisitively; others gave the odd backward glance. Time to leave... He fled and made his way to the surface-vehicle... It was time to meet the great mutant mind....

The thirty-minute journey passed in a flash. Marcus pulled up to the side of a small hut. It was isolated, several miles from the city centre. Nothing but barren Martian sand surrounded it. He stepped out of the surface-vehicle and made his way towards the open door. He halted. Suddenly, he heard footsteps, and a face slowly emerged. A small, bald mutant dressed in white stood at the foot of the door. His left hand was badly disfigured. It was swollen, with only three fingers visible. His skin was golden, and his nose was broad and flat.

"Marcus Harlan... the great time traveller. We've been expecting you..."

Marcus didn't reply. He stood somewhat perturbed as a cool Martian wind ruffled his hair.

"My name's Solon. Please enter." Marcus entered and followed the diminutive mutant through the small pale coloured hallway. They reached a room.

"Please Marcus..." said Solon, his disfigured hand directing him through.

Marcus stepped in somewhat apprehensively, and his eyes immediately focused on another mutant who sat on the floor almost in a meditative state... Democritus! He too was bald, and dressed in white, his skin golden in colour. His head was quite large, larger than the average mutant; the extended larger frontal area of the skull stood out boldly, indicating a highly intelligent systematic brain, highly developed cognitive faculties, greater conceptual capacity, Marcus thought. He knew he was in the right company by visual analysis alone.

"Mr Harlan, please come sit...My name's Democritus..." His ancient eyes shone like two dark pearls, ablaze with a fiery energy, an energy that appeared to consume the actual organ of sight itself.

Marcus followed this instruction without reply. He sat facing him and noticed that he too had a disfigured hand; his right hand. Only two fingers were visible. Marcus said, "Solon tells me that I was expected. What does he mean by that?"

"My disciple Solon merely applied the obvious…"

"You had a premonition…?"

"Marcus most premonitions can be explained by coincidence. Even the most improbable events will occur if you wait long enough. The laws of chance do not merely permit coincidence they compel them. It's mathematical certainty, probability, statistics. Regardless, this has nothing to do with premonitions, I assure you. The simple truth is, any man that travels ahead in time like you have… a great time pioneer, would inevitably develop deep profound philosophical thoughts. After such an incredible metaphysical experience his mind would never be the same. He would naturally want to discover more, have questions answered. There's no one better than me, here on Mars, to answer such questions. Logic dictates that through the natural course of time you would come here eventually…"

Silence fell…

Marcus lipped his lips and said, "I met a certain Dr Madani. It was he that led me to you. He gave me your contact details, hence my presence here. He said he has known you for several years."

"Yes, that's correct…"

Marcus rubbed his eyes then said, "He tells me that you have great knowledge…"

"Knowledge…" Democritus smiled as the word rolled out from his mouth. "It means to acquire information, and to process that information accordingly, using the brain. Reason and logic automatically help us to understand the data acquired. Every human being attains a certain amount of knowledge as he or she goes through the journey of life; some at greater levels, others at lower levels. But the knowledge I possess, is inbuilt within the DNA. That is, I'm genetically predisposed to knowledge and geniality. It's a knowledge that is not acquired as such but is inbuilt at a cellular level. So, tell me...what can I help you with?"

"Democritus, ever since I returned to natural time, I have developed powers to see into the future. This power is manifested in the form of visions... I can't explain why I've developed this gift, but I have."

"Marcus a human being is a very complicated animal... We are a nexus of electromagnetic forces... The mind is the most complicated piece of matter within the universe...There are one set of laws for the mind and another set for matter. Mind is a power in the universe. The mind can achieve things that are simply not allowed for in the accepted scientific scheme, which is basically a physicalistic picture of reality." He paused... "It's as if a metaphysical doorway has opened within your mind, and your brain now resonates at a different frequency. It's as if your mind operates outside of the three dimensions of space and the one dimension of time, the four-dimensional world of space-time... beyond this physical reality." He took a deep breath almost as if he were about to mediate... "Now, tell me about your visions Marcus... All I want to know from you is what you saw. I won't ask you any sensitive questions. I realize it's a very delicate sensitive situation."

There was a moment of deep silence...

Marcus said, "I've had four visions so far. Three have already taken place the other is yet to come... I can't control them. It's as if space and time open up before me and the world that I know fades for a time. Then images suddenly appear in an oscillating haze...yet clear. In my first vision I witnessed the death of my friend and his son. Both perished with all on board when their spaceship suddenly exploded in outer space, spaceflight 101...Mars to Titan journey...In the vision, I saw the ship leaving Mars. I also saw all the passengers seated in the ship. I even saw the two pilots...the control-room. Then destruction followed. The next day this dreadful event took place. In vision two...I saw the destruction of a building. It was a Hindu convention. Many Hindus died in New Oslo. Again, this horrible event took place, and was later confirmed on the news. As for vision three, it was the earthquake on planet earth in the city of Osaka, Japan... Again, it actually ended up taking place. It was also confirmed on the news."

"And as for vision four?"

Marcus eyes suddenly became distant, as if recollecting a blurred memory...

"In vision four, which took place this morning, I saw a man standing outside on an open elevated platform giving a speech to a crowd of thousands. I couldn't hear anything, only see! He was dressed in black... It was..." he paused as if something had gripped him suddenly at the throat...

"It was who?" asked Democritus.

"The politician Larry Schneider... Images of destruction followed. I saw riots taking place, death and destruction everywhere. Next I saw the people of Mars being implanted with Nano-chips... These chips were inserted into the brain, near the temporal lobe. I could actually see the signals, low frequency radio waves being sent out from a central base on Mars. Basic logic told me that these signals were able to collect all cephalic data, every thought and emotion via the chips which had the capacity to store all the necessary neurological information; a mind control society!! Hacking into the human mind requires decoding the logic of neurons.... This evil power in the future to come, via the tyrant Schneider, will have all the technological power to do so.... Finally, I saw Larry Schneider standing in a room accompanied by another person whose face was hidden by the haze. He sat in a large brown chair dressed in black and his hand was placed on a button. He faced a large rectangular screen. Next I saw images of Planet Earth pictured across this screen. A jungle, a desert, various cities, great mountains, oceans...Then, I heard the word, 'fire...' The button was then pressed by the man whose face was hidden by the blur and haze of the vision. After that I could see a vast array of huge Earth-destroying bombs being launched into outer space...deep space. Next I could see a series of devastating explosions taking place on Planet Earth. Many perished...! Then, once the vision ceased, I decided to drive into town... As I entered the busy

THE MARS TIME-PROJECT

town centre of Olympus, I saw a crowd gathering. To my utter astonishment I then saw that very person, Larry Schneider with his small group of twisted followers, disciples if you like, all dressed in black being interviewed by the Mars News team. What are the odds of this occurring directly after my revelation? It's as if a greater force is guiding me to my destiny... my mission. I headed towards the crowd, towards Schneider drawn by some magnetic attraction. Then, the crowd that surrounded him turned and rushed over towards me. They all recognized me as the historic time-traveller. Many were jubilant. Then, Larry Schneider approached... The very man that I have come to understand that I must kill, stood almost face to face with me. How bizarre is that? He then said and I remember it vividly, as if it were etched into my mind... *'We appear to pull the same crowd Marcus Harlan...you a pioneer, the first man to travel ahead in time and me, well let's just say the people like what I have to say. It seems that the same destiny awaits us. I could do with a man like you. Your name is echoing throughout the solar system. You've made history...Martian history as the first great time-traveller. You could do much for me at a political level. We could do great things together....'* He then gave me his card with his contact details in the hope that I contact him. How ironic! Indeed, a certain destiny does await us! We exchanged a few more words, and then I departed, and made my way here to you... Can you believe that Democritus? It blew my mind."

"Democritus gazed deeply into his eyes and said... "A bizarre sequence of events to say the least... Regardless Marcus, this vision of the future is one that leaves you with great responsibility."

Marcus's eyes widened with sudden surprise, as some key inside him turned... "So, you believe me then?"

"Marcus, please.... Consider the following: when atoms are broken down, quarks and electrons are discovered, and within these particles, exists pure energy which is not physically measurable. This energy has its own intelligence, its own mind if you like... Every human being is connected to the universe, a giant cosmic soup. Every human being experiences the reality of being the centre of their own universe... Therefore, everything we believe and think, does not just govern our behaviour... it literally creates and shapes the world we experience. Furthermore, the solidity of the world seems totally indisputable as a fixed thing that you can touch and see, however modern physics tells us that this solidity is a mirage... that is, all physical matter is a result of a frequency, and what that means is.... if you amplify the frequency, the structure of matter will change."

"Please forgive me Democritus, but what does that have to do with what I've just asked you?"

"Marcus... what I've just stated doesn't necessarily connect or correlate with your question as such. But the meaning and moral behind it is this... once you've understood that this universe is beyond human comprehension, so complex, and that the nature of reality and so forth strays into the sphere that is beyond physical understanding, why would I have a problem accepting your story? Everything that surrounds us is peppered with mystery. Thus, I believe you Marcus...Not to mention that I read your eyes like no other. I can almost see pictures formed within them as I stare. It's as if your brain transmits all thought across your retina, declaring all.... You speak the truth Marcus. You have acquired a gift. A very special gift...There is no doubt in my mind that you are a prophet. Your visions declare it so to my senses and deep intuition. It verifies all..."

Marcus sat there totally absorbed by what he was hearing and said, "I can't tell you how relieved I am to hear this! This leads me to share this with you..." Marcus paused and summoned courage. "Democritus, Larry Schneider needs to be stopped... The future of Mars and Earth now lie in my hands. Kill one man to save the lives of millions... I may have to face the consequences, but I need to rid Mars of this evil tyrant regardless...I'll be remembered as the first time-traveller...a great pioneer, and if caught, a murderer too..."

"Yes Marcus, he must be stopped at all costs. You have no choice. Remember morality and ethics must be grounded in logic. Thus, the logical thing to do, in this particular situation, is to kill him for the sake of Mars and Earth...This man is pure evil...reptilian DNA! There's an obvious abnormality, malfunction within the reptilian complex...his brain."

"What do you mean?"

"Marcus, evil doesn't exist as a spirit being or an entity, like many religions teach. Evil only exists within the soul of Man as an acting potential within the reptilian complex. An overactive reptilian complex, as in the case of Larry Schneider, brings out the worst in Man, dominance, territoriality, aggression...pure evil...!"

"I see...!"

"Now, if this mission of yours is planned out well...you will escape the authorities and come out clean. Believe me, you won't be caught, but you need a good solid strategic plan, and that plan needs to be executed with great precision and care. Remember, you actually met Larry Schneider today and have his contact details. It makes things a lot easier for you Marcus. The Gods are on your side..."

There was a moment of Silence...

Marcus then said, "Democritus, I want to tell my wife Charlotte about this vision too…"

"No," the philosopher snapped with finality. "My strict advice to you is, do not share this with your wife. Keep it secret from her. It's best…It will be too much for her to deal with. This must remain strictly between us."

"Okay Democritus, I take your point," he replied. "I did however tell her about the other visions, but this last one will remain between us. I won't say a word to her…"

"Good Marcus…Now listen to me, come back tomorrow so I can help you formulate a plan. We will talk more. Solon will see you out…"

Marcus stood up and turned, his eyes now glowing with an inner assurance that they had initially lacked… He had support. This gave him a greater push to see out his mission, his destiny…

"Please Marcus, follow me…" said Solon raising his disfigured hand. His voice trailed off into silence…

That night found Marcus sitting alone in his hut. Hours had passed. He had been thinking deeply...thinking about Larry Schneider. 'I must kill him...he needs to be stopped for the sake of Mars...Earth,' he mumbled. He then checked the time and wondered when Charlotte would be back. She had spent the whole day with Aurora. Aurora certainly needed the company, especially after the devastation of losing both husband and son. He made his way for the door and stood outside gazing towards the Martian horizon. Mars was beautiful he thought, and he would see that it remained that way. He clenched his fists! His knuckles whitened. Dust swirled around him blown by a gust of wind... He wondered whether he would have a vision of the assassination itself, and the events that would follow. He started to walk; eyes fixed. The stars were packed overhead in astonishing numbers. They looked like sparks... Then, suddenly he felt dizzy. Blackness swirled around him distorting all vision for a moment. He fell to the ground as if hit by a bolt of force. He gazed towards the Martian atmosphere, the Martian night sky as if dead, then, that same oscillating haze appeared before him cancelling out the view of the nocturnal sky. He fell into a timeless state. Images started to form, shimmering into existence. With dreamlike precision he could see Larry Schneider again dressed in black standing in that room. He could also see that other person, whose face was still hidden. He was sitting in that same large brown chair dressed in black and his hand was placed on that red button, just like before. He saw the same large rectangular screen. Images of Planet Earth were pictured again...Then, he heard the word, 'fire...' It was almost a replay of the vision he'd had previously. The button was pressed by the obscured face...devastation would follow. He could now see Larry Schneider grinning, eyes igniting with sheer evil. Suddenly, the blur and haze that masked the face of the other person parted. Slowly its features resolved to reveal its identity for the first time. Marcus' mouth opened in horror and his eyes widened in shock. He lay on the ground in devastation and disbelief, a great despairing sob ballooning from the pit of his stomach. Cold terror cut through him like a knife. The man sitting there on the large brown chair dressed in black was Marcus Harlan...!

Lightning Source UK Ltd.
Milton Keynes UK
UKHW010950080223
416610UK00015B/1855

9 781845 497514